By Royal Appointment

You're invited to a royal wedding!

*From turreted castles to picturesque palaces,
these kingdoms may be steeped in tradition,
but romance always rules!*

*So don't miss your VIP invite to the most
extravagant weddings of the year!*

Your royal carriage awaits. . . .

Coming next month:
A Royal Marriage of Convenience
by
Marion Lennox,
only from Harlequin Romance®.

Dear Reader,

Josie in *English Lord, Ordinary Lady* is definitely a modern woman. She lives life to the fullest, from the roots of her bright pink hair to the tips of her bejeweled toes, and plays by her own rules. That is until stuffy, conventional Will arrives on the scene. Suddenly, not only is the future of her home and her job in jeopardy, but also the freedom she's fought so hard to maintain.

Writing Will and Josie's story was an absolute blast! Josie was so naughty sometimes, I found myself giggling as I typed. And then there was Will. Good, solid, dependable Will. He didn't stand a chance! I loved watching him lose his starchiness as Josie got under his skin.

English Lord, Ordinary Lady is all about learning to embrace history at the same time as planning for a bright, fresh and exciting future. I'm really proud to be a Harlequin Romance® author, following in the footsteps of so many well-loved and respected authors, while at the same time being able to write stories with my own fresh take on boy-meets-girl. Let's face it—a good romance is never going to go out of fashion!

Fiona Harper

FIONA HARPER
English Lord, Ordinary Lady

By Royal Appointment

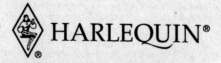

TORONTO • NEW YORK • LONDON
AMSTERDAM • PARIS • SYDNEY • HAMBURG
STOCKHOLM • ATHENS • TOKYO • MILAN • MADRID
PRAGUE • WARSAW • BUDAPEST • AUCKLAND

ISBN-13: 978-0-373-18353-1
ISBN-10:   0-373-18353-4

ENGLISH LORD, ORDINARY LADY

First North American Publication 2008.

This edition published by arrangement with Harlequin Books S.A.

® and TM are trademarks of the publisher. Trademarks indicated with ® are registered in the United States Patent and Trademark Office, the Canadian Trade Marks Office and in other countries.

www.eHarlequin.com

Printed in U.S.A.

Fiona Harper was constantly teased as a child for either having her nose in a book or for living in a dream world. Things haven't changed much since then, but at least in writing she's found a use for her runaway imagination.

After studying dance at university, Fiona worked as a dancer, teacher and choreographer before trading that career in for video editing and production. When she became a mother she cut back on her working hours to spend time with her children, and when her littlest one started preschool Fiona found a few spare moments to rediscover an old, but not forgotten, love—writing.

Fiona lives in London, but her other favorite places to be are the Highlands of Scotland and the Kent countryside on a summer's afternoon. She loves cooking good food and anything cinnamon-flavored. Of course, she still can't keep away from a good book or a good movie—especially romances—but only if she's stocked up with tissues, because she knows she will need them by the end, be it happy or sad. Her favorite things in the world are her wonderful husband, who has learned to decipher her incoherent ramblings, and her two daughters. Visit Fiona at her Web site, www.fionaharper.com.

For Norina, not my only cheerleader,
but certainly my loudest!

CHAPTER ONE

WILL stopped the car and got out, leaving it slap-bang in the middle of the road. He left the door hanging open and walked forward a few steps.

The turrets and chimneys on Elmhurst Hall rose above the surrounding trees, its sandstone walls warmed to a golden yellow by the slanting afternoon sun. Long-paned windows filled the stonework and high arches curved over the heavy wooden doors.

This was the moment he'd been waiting for since he'd opened the letter from the solicitor a month ago. The moment his family had anticipated for three generations. If he failed—uncharacteristic for him, but not impossible—it could take another three generations to recover. An eventuality he was not prepared to contemplate.

He got back into the car and glanced at the publicity brochure on the passenger seat. It said that Elmhurst Hall was 'a vision from a fairy tale'. At the time, he'd just thought that was sales talk.

He took a deep breath and gazed through the windscreen. It was more than a vision. It was breathtaking.

And now it belonged to him.

He turned the key in the ignition and drove down the country lane towards the hall, keeping at an even twenty miles an hour. It was just as well there was no other traffic, because he was hogging the road completely.

He brought the car to a halt as he reached the large wrought-iron gates. They were more than ten feet high and were bolted shut—probably to keep the peasants like him out. The thought only made him smile again. Too bad. He was here now, and there was nothing the rest of the Radcliffe family could do to stop him.

Now he was closer, the grandeur of the building faded a little. Gutters hanging off and crumbling stonework made her seem like a tired old movie star, past her heyday, but with the echoes of her former beauty still visible beneath.

He smiled. How ironic that the grandson of the family outcast might just have enough money and skill to give this old lady the nip and tuck she needed. It was obvious that the late Lord Radcliffe hadn't had either the cash or the inclination to do so.

What a waste. He'd found old buildings in a much worse state of repair and seen them restored so that no one would guess they'd ever lost their fairy-tale quality. He'd built a business on it. Now he would just have to work his magic here.

Down to his left was a small road. He followed it and found himself in a large and rather empty visitor car park.

The way back towards the hall was through a large walled garden. He checked his watch. Mr Barrett was expecting him at four o'clock and it was almost five to. He'd better get a move-on. Two tugs at a rickety-looking gate covered in peeling green paint gave him entrance to the garden. It wasn't the big open space he'd expected; it was divided into much smaller sections by thick yew hedges.

After five minutes of going this way and that, he decided there was no logic to the layout. He reached a crossroads and considered his options. The path ahead of him seemed to be the obvious choice to take him to the hall, but he knew from the experience of the last five minutes that nothing in this place was as it seemed.

He was just about to take the path on his left when a creature with shimmering wings burst from the shrubbery and landed on the path in front of him. 'A vision from a fairy tale' the brochure had said. Still, he hadn't expected to see *actual* fairies. His feet were frozen to the spot while his heart galloped on ahead.

Before he could rub his eyes, another figure tumbled from the foliage and landed spread-eagled on the path. Laughter, light and musical like bursting bubbles, filled the air. The sound vanished abruptly as the pair noticed they weren't alone. Two pairs of impish eyes fixed themselves on him.

Will stared back, his senses still reeling from the sudden assault of noise and colour.

The little one with wings spoke first.

'Who are you?'

He stared at the protuberances on her back. They were made of pink netting and were held in place by a criss-cross of elastic stretched over a fur-trimmed coat.

'I'm Will,' he said, then wondered why he hadn't introduced himself properly. He never forgot his manners.

She stood up and brushed the dirt from her sticky-out skirt.

'I'm Harriet,' she said and offered him a pink-gloved hand to shake. Will bent forward and took it, too surprised by the gesture to think of doing anything else.

He had no idea how to gauge the age of a little girl. It was something that came with experience he didn't have. Older than three—her speech was clear and lisp-free—but probably younger than seven. He didn't know why knowing how old she was seemed important. Maybe because he needed a concrete fact to ground this rather surreal meeting in reality.

'Hattie, I've told you not to talk to strangers unless I say it's OK.'

Will registered the voice—it was older, but just as clear and precise. He meant to take a good look at the fairy's older companion, but his gaze was locked with the little girl's.

He'd never seen such an intense stare in his life before—not unless he counted looking in the mirror. And she didn't shy away or hide behind the other girl's legs as he would have expected. Instead she fixed him with a regal look of superiority and met his curious gaze. Finally, when she'd got the measure of him, she gave a nod of recognition.

How odd. Children rarely warmed to him. He always felt so stiff and awkward in their presence. But this strange little girl didn't seem to mind that.

The noise of the other person getting to her feet drew his attention. Her gaze was just as intense as her friend's. Although his senses were back on track and he was now fully aware that she was nothing more than human, he couldn't quite shake the feeling that there was something different about her.

He shifted his weight onto his other foot.

'The hall is closed to visitors on Thursdays and Fridays until April,' she said. 'How did you get in?'

Will glanced briefly in the direction of the car park. 'I came in through the gate, of course. I have an appointment with Mr Barrett.' The man was supposed to be the butler, or something like that. He hadn't known that real butlers still existed.

She held out her hand for Hattie's.

'You'd better follow me, then. This section of the gardens is divided into "rooms", as the gardener likes to put it. It can be a little confusing if you don't know your way around.'

Hattie skipped next to the older girl, who he was now suspecting might be a babysitter rather than a sibling. A multicoloured striped hat that reminded him of a tea cosy with strange pink tassels on either side was pulled down over her ears and she wore a short denim jacket over cargo trousers and clumpy boots.

He shrugged. Who was he to judge? It was turning

out to be a much more practical choice of outfit than his Italian suit as they trudged along the pathways between the hedges. Mud was already clinging to the hems of his trousers and clogging his shoes.

They entered a large sunken garden filled with vast flowerbeds and a fountain in the centre and at last he had a clear view of the back of Elmhurst Hall.

He knew enough about architecture to recognise that the building was a patchwork of different periods and styles, some sections dating back to the sixteenth century.

The wing facing the front gates had obviously been added later, the grand façade, but round the back of the building one could see the history. Different sections had been added by previous owners, all wanting to improve Elmhurst Hall and leave their fingerprint on it. Now it was his turn to do the same.

It truly was a unique piece of architecture. He could hardly wait to start exploring it.

A small set of fingers tugged his hand then wiggled their way into his palm until they were clasped in his.

'Come on, Will. It's this way.'

Hattie pulled him in the direction of a set of stairs that went through a small square tower. The path then continued upwards and across a spacious flat lawn, ending at a large wooden door that was big enough to squash him flat if it fell off its hinges. He let the little girl drag him forwards, too caught up in absorbing his surroundings to navigate his own way.

The babysitter was standing in the arch of the

tower, frowning down at him as he climbed the steps. He turned to Hattie.

'So, if visitors aren't allowed today, what are *you* doing here?'

'Playing princesses and trolls.'

Her voice was flat and matter-of-fact, as if she expected every visitor to engage in similar activities. 'I'm the princess,' she said, spreading her full skirt slightly to emphasise the fact, 'and Mummy is the troll.'

There was a small grunt from the figure at the top of the stairs. 'Mummy always ends up being the troll.'

She was the child's mother? Will took a closer look as he climbed towards her. She barely looked older than a teenager herself. Maybe it was her height. She was petite, reaching five feet three at the very most.

The hand she thrust out for Hattie's was more an order than a request. Hattie slipped her gloved fingers from his and ran to her mother.

Something about him put this woman on the defensive. He could see it in the stubborn set of her chin, the way she avoided eye contact. She started off again before he'd caught up, always keeping a good distance between them.

He followed her, not through the large wooden door in front of them, but round the side of the building into an area that would have been the servants' entrance in days gone by. Hattie broke free and disappeared through a little door, leaving it open behind her.

The woman turned to look at him.

'What are you really doing here?' he said, his

usually sharp and inquisitive mind finally whirring away like normal.

She shrugged. 'Like Hattie said, we were playing. You couldn't find a better place to play imaginary games than here.'

Yes, but there were more suitable ways to go about it than trespassing in the grounds of Elmhurst Hall. He was about to say as much, but downgraded his observation to something less confrontational. 'You have the owner's permission?'

She nodded. 'In a roundabout way. I work and live here. Use of the grounds is one of the perks of the job.'

Well, he'd find out more about that later.

She nodded in the direction of the open door.

'Good luck,' she said, without any hint of encouragement in her eyes. 'You're not the first man in a suit to turn up. You're wasting your time, though. When Lord Radcliffe died...' Here she paused, and her voice softened slightly. She shook her head once, as if to swish away an uninvited thought, and continued. 'I'm guessing you'll go away empty-handed. There's precious little left to pay his debts.'

Now he could study her face properly, he could see why he'd thought she was only a child. She had large eyes and ripe lips set in an elfin face. If it weren't for that square little chin, she'd look just like a fairy—timeless, ageless, wise.

'Thank you for your advice...'

She blinked at him.

'Josie.' As she said her name she reached up and grabbed the tea-cosy hat with one hand.

'I'm not here to…' The rest of his sentence was forgotten as he realised the bright pink tassels didn't move with the rest of that hat. He squinted at her then opened his eyes wide.

Not tassels. Plaits! Little stubby braids in a particularly violent shade of fuchsia.

This woman was one surprise after another.

He saw the barest of smiles touch her lips as she turned and stepped over the threshold. She liked the fact she'd shocked him, made him forget what he was going to say.

Well, two could play at that game. And he had a feeling his arrival here was going to cause a bigger upset than discovering an employee with pink hair. If his instincts were right they'd be as surprised as if they'd…well, found fairies at the bottom of the garden.

The narrow passageways in the servants' quarters amplified the footsteps of the stranger walking behind her. Josie turned to knock on a door made in a century when people must have been a heck of a lot shorter.

At five-two, she wasn't going to have a problem, but Will Whatever-his-name-was was going to have to duck.

She sighed as she ushered the visitor in to see Barrett and closed the door behind him. She had no wish to hear what he had to say. It was all far too depressing.

Harry had been the dearest, sweetest old man

alive, but he'd been hopeless with money. She'd suspected it ever since she'd come to live here six years ago, but only his death and the unravelling of his haphazard accounts had proved how bad things really were.

They were all in limbo until the legal wrangling over Harry's estate was over. He'd once told her he would leave her the cottage she lived in, but in all the rooms full of clutter Harry had left behind no one had come across anything resembling a will.

That left her and Hattie at the mercy of the new owner. Her beloved godfather had let her live in the run-down cottage virtually rent-free and she couldn't see the new Lord Radcliffe honouring that. He'd not only inherited the hall, which ate money with a voracious appetite, but also all of Harry's debts. Even if he was inclined to help out, he probably wouldn't be able to afford to.

Her salary from running the tearoom here only just about covered her basic outgoings. If she had to pay rent of any kind, the only option would be to cut out Hattie's activities, and even then there'd be a huge shortfall.

She grimaced as she threaded her way through the ancient corridors towards the kitchen—for that was undoubtedly where her daughter had run off to. Hattie loved her ballet lessons and she would sulk for a month if she had to stop.

Personally, Josie couldn't see what all the fuss was about. There was no freedom in it, no exuberance. Twisting yourself into unnatural positions and stuffing your feet into hard little shoes that were two sizes too small. No way.

Still, Hattie seemed to like torture in a tutu and Josie wasn't about to stop her doing what she loved. That was what good parents did—they supported their children's choices and let them blossom into the unique creatures they were meant to be. She was not going to impose her own likes and dislikes on her daughter as if they were the Ten Commandments.

Just as she'd predicted, Hattie was sitting at the kitchen table looking expectantly at Mrs Barrett, Elmhurst's cook. And just as her husband would answer to nothing other than "Barrett", Mrs Barrett was conveniently deaf unless she was addressed as "Cook" by most people. Josie got away with *Mrs B*, but only if she wasn't being too cheeky and the older woman was in the right kind of mood.

'And will it be your usual, Miss Hattie?'

Josie smiled. This was a game they played, Cook and Hattie. She thought it reminded the loyal servant of the glory days of the hall when she'd had staff to boss around and 'at-homes' to cater for.

There were no prizes for guessing why Hattie liked the game. It was every girl's dream, wasn't it? To be Cinderella or Sleeping Beauty and live in a castle. And she wasn't going to stop Hattie having her dreams, even if she knew the reality was pretty grim.

Most people didn't realise this, but living in a fantasy castle could drain a girl's spirit. It wouldn't be long before she'd go stir-crazy. She'd start snoozing all day, or losing her shoes, and do a Rapunzel—grow her hair so she could get the heck out of the stuffy old mausoleum.

Hattie folded her hands on her lap. 'Yes, please, Cook.'

'And can I tempt you with a freshly baked gingersnap to go with that?'

Josie tried hard not to laugh as Hattie considered the offer, her head tipped to one side, eyes focused on the ceiling. She looked so prim and proper sitting there, her back perfectly straight and her ankles crossed.

'I think I would like that very much, Cook.'

Mrs B nodded and poured Hattie's juice into a delicate little teacup, complete with saucer, reserved exclusively for that use.

'Hi, Mrs B,' said Josie, ruffling her daughter's hair. The action was rewarded with a scowl as Hattie removed her tiara and smoothed down the fluffy bits.

'Afternoon, dear. Catch any trolls today?'

Josie chuckled and slid into the chair opposite Hattie. 'Not exactly.'

Cook gave her a quizzical look as she placed a mug of tea in front of her.

Hattie was happy to fill in the gaps. 'We met a man in the gardens. His name is Will. I think he likes fairies,' she said through a mouthful of biscuit crumbs.

'I took him in to see Barrett,' Josie added. 'Not that he'll have much joy until the new lord is traced. Even then he's going to have to join the back of a very long queue if he wants his money.'

Mrs Barrett parked her ample bottom in the chair next to her. 'Barrett told me today that they've found him. Working overseas, he said. The late Lord Radcliffe's great-nephew. Apparently he will be arriving some time this week. There's an emergency staff meeting at four-thirty. I'll look after Hattie while you go. Barrett can fill me in later.'

Josie took a sip of her tea. 'I didn't think Edward Radcliffe had any sons. I thought you told me he gave up trying after four daughters.'

'No, Edward was Lord Radcliffe's youngest brother. The new lord's grandfather would have been the middle of the three Radcliffe brothers.'

'I never knew there was another Radcliffe brother. I don't remember seeing anything in the genealogy.'

'No, well, you wouldn't. It happened long before you were born, Josie. Some big family falling-out between Harry's father and his youngest son. The whole family disowned him. The man the solicitors hired discovered that he'd changed his name, which explains why his descendants have been so hard to trace.'

Josie gave a wry smile. 'Another black sheep, then.'

Mrs B just changed the subject. 'You'd better hurry along or you'll be late for the meeting.'

Josie leaned back in her chair, kicked her booted feet up to rest on the table and ignored the disapproving stare she got from the other two. 'I've got a few minutes left. Time to drink my tea, at any rate.'

So, the black sheep's grandson had inherited Elmhurst. There was no doubting that life at the hall had fallen into a rut as deep as the Cheddar Gorge. It could do with a good shake-up.

Only she didn't want some Hooray Henry storming into her territory and causing a ruckus. If there was going to be an uproar, she'd jolly well cause it herself.

Josie returned from the staff meeting feeling a little foolish. Scratch that; she felt a whole lot foolish. Not that she'd let Will Whatever-his-name-was see how she was feeling.

She stomped back to the kitchen. How dared he walk in here, looking all ordinary? He wasn't what she'd been expecting at all. Anyway, it was his own fault she'd been a bit off with him. He shouldn't go sneaking up on people in the gardens and expect them to know who he was.

It was still niggling her the following Monday morning as she was preparing the display of cakes for the tearoom with Mrs B.

'Who is this guy, anyway? And where did he go after the meeting on Friday? He hasn't been around all weekend.'

Mrs B sighed and carried on cutting a carrot cake into even slices.

'Barrett says he's a businessman of some sort, quite successful too, by all accounts.'

'What kind of business, that's what I want to know?' Josie muttered to herself. Mrs B shrugged and placed the newly carved cake into the display case. Her baked goods were the most popular things on sale in the tearoom.

'Oh, something to do with old buildings,' Mrs B replied.

There was no point in pursuing this line of questioning further. To the loyal cook he was Lord Radcliffe, and that was that.

Nobody knew anything about him. Old buildings. That could mean anything. He could be a property developer planning to raze the hall to the ground and build a horrible modern housing estate.

Josie wiped her hands on a tea towel and took her apron off. 'I'm off to the cash-and-carry to stock up on crisps and suchlike. I should be back before noon.'

Mrs B nodded and returned to arranging a tray of muffins in a pleasing manner. Josie put her coat on, pulled a stripy hat out of the pocket and plonked it on her head, tucking her hair behind her ears.

She drove through the village of Elmhurst and joined the main road that would take her to the nearby town of Groombridge. After she'd loaded up the boot of the old Morris Minor with provisions for the tearoom, she decided to take a little detour. Not exactly work-related, but it was in the interests of all those employed at the hall, so it almost counted.

The public library was only a five-minute walk away. She ignored the rows of books and headed straight for one of the computer terminals where she could get internet access. It was conveniently ready at the home page of a search engine and she sat down and typed in *William Roberts* with two fingers. She'd finally learnt his surname from Barrett.

Almost instantly a long list popped up. She discounted the first few—results from family history sites—and scanned down the list. A very long list.

The first site she tried was the cyber-home of William Roberts, die-hard fishing enthusiast. She smiled as she closed the page and looked for another link. She'd always thought that once you'd seen one picture of a dead fish, you'd seen them all. Obviously not.

The next try was more like it. It wasn't exactly what she was looking for, but it had a link to another site and when she followed that she hit gold.

Her worst fears were confirmed.

The link brought up a news article. It seemed that only months ago, Will had picked up an award for one of his projects. The brief blurb underneath the photograph described his company as one that took on both restoration projects and property development.

She rested her head in her hands and massaged her scalp with her fingers. It was as if she could feel the structure of her life crumbling away. If Elmhurst Hall closed, her only option would be to go home and live with her parents. And she'd always said it would be a cold day in hell before that happened.

She navigated to a different page, hoping to garner a little more information on the mysterious Mr Roberts. The site only gave the most basic information, but she could see that he'd done very well for himself, building his company up from virtually nothing.

Out of the blue, she heard her mother's voice echo in her head: 'He might be rich, darling. But he's hardly one of us, is he?'

Her mother was such a snob.

'He's a bit dishy, isn't he?'

Josie turned to find Marianne, the librarian, looking over her shoulder. The silence rule was never going to be upheld very well while Marianne worked here. Somehow, a place of serious contemplation and study had turned into a hotbed of gossip. And Marianne was the main culprit.

'I hadn't really noticed, actually.'

Marianne whacked her on the shoulder with a paperback. 'Go on! You can't fool me. Look at that lovely thick dark hair and those brooding, serious eyes. I bet there's a fine physique underneath that suit.'

'Marianne, you've been spending far too long camped out in the spicier parts of the romance section. Not every woman thinks about a man in terms of hard abs and strong thighs. Some things are more important.'

Marianne hissed out a laugh. 'Yeah, right! Just don't dribble too much on that keyboard, OK?'

Josie turned back to face the monitor, closed down the page and stood up, whisking her belongings under her arm as she did so.

'Nobody here is going to be doing any drooling, trust me.'

'Whatever you say, Josie.'

The librarian sauntered off, a smug grin on her

face. Josie sighed. Even if she wanted to—which she didn't—she wasn't going to let herself think about moody looks and washboard abs. Those didn't count for anything. A man with a heart and a soul was a much rarer, and infinitely more precious, commodity.

Will Roberts might look 'dishy' but he might also be the worst thing to happen to Elmhurst Hall in five centuries. And there was absolutely nothing she could do about it.

CHAPTER TWO

WILL sat in the corner of the tearoom, partly hidden by a hideous piece of garden trellis with faded plastic ivy poking through it. He picked up a leaf that had either fallen off or been picked off by a bored customer and fixed it back onto one of the many waiting stubs.

Something would have to be done about this place.

While the hall looked elegantly shabby at present, the tearoom just looked cheap.

The only possible problem might be its manageress. He'd been here a month—well, not an entire month. Only weekends, really—and he still had no idea how she'd react to the news that he wanted to completely gut and refurbish the tearoom. In the end, he'd had to cut short his work in London and come down here on a Monday afternoon.

You'd think the pink-haired girl would be pleased he was bringing this beautiful place back to life, but every time he was in her presence it was as if he could hear her tutting at him. Not out loud, of course. But the noise was there all the same. Inside his head.

He watched her as she chatted to customers, and, clearing their plates, said goodbye. She might look a little strange, but she was good with people. Warm. Engaging. With *other* people.

He checked his watch. Only five more minutes and the tearoom would close. Then she'd have to talk to him.

Over the last few weeks he'd met with all the staff, one by one, to talk through their jobs and find out if they had ideas for improvement. And, while he'd listened carefully to each one of them, he hadn't been convinced about some of the ideas. Especially Molly's. She was one of the more enthusiastic volunteer guides. Somehow, a garden-gnome museum didn't sit right with his vision for the hall. It needed ideas with taste, class—initiatives with a certain sense of respect for tradition and the history of the place.

He wiggled another leaf on the ivy trail and pushed it back into position. Totally fake and out of place.

A cup of tea clattered onto the table in front of him. He looked up to find Josie staring at him. *Let's get it over with, then*, her expression said.

'Thank you. Why don't you sit down?'

She looked away for a split-second then dropped into the moulded plastic seat bolted onto the metal supports that held the table in place.

'I've been looking over the accounts for the tearooms.'

She let out a breath through her nostrils and continued staring at him.

'They're not good—'

She leaned back in her seat and crossed her arms. 'I do as well as I can under the circumstances. You try running a place like this with only one working oven, not enough staff and a budget that only allows for the cheapest, lowest-quality ingredients. I'd like to see you do better.'

'I said the figures weren't good. I didn't say they were terrible. In fact, if you'd let me finish, I was about to say that the tearoom seems to be the only part of the estate that's made any money in the last few years and, reading between the lines, I'd say that had an awful lot to do with you.'

Her arms dropped to her sides. 'Oh.'

'I'm not going to beat around the bush, Josie. You're producing a great menu under severe limitations, but this place is a dive.'

Her body straightened and her hands flew to her hips, but then she looked around the room, her eyes lingering on the ivy, and she slumped again.

'You're right. It's hideous. I told Harry that over and over, but he wouldn't hear of changing anything. Couldn't see what the problem was.'

He took a sip of his tea. It was hot and strong and exactly how he liked it.

'So, you won't have any objections to a bit of re-furbishment, then?'

'A bit? I'd say we ought to rip the whole lot out and start again!' She jumped off the chair. 'Just look at this.'

He almost choked on his tea as she ran to get a

wooden chair from near the till, balanced it on the table next to him and vaulted onto the table-top.

Circus tricks? What the heck was she doing?

Unfortunately his legs seemed to be half-wedged under the plastic table and he wasn't about to go anywhere fast.

'Josie! I don't think you should…'

She made a dismissive noise. 'I'm not very heavy. It'll be fine.'

Finally his leg came free and he lurched forward trying to grab hold of her. Too late. She was atop the chair and poking at the polystyrene-tiled suspended ceiling.

There was nothing else to do but join her on top of the table and hope the plastic was stronger than it looked.

'See?'

'Josie, I…'

And then he did see. Beyond the polystyrene tile she had moved was the original ceiling, beams and all. It was dark and dusty now but if it were restored it would look sensational.

She was smiling down at him. Even standing on the chair she wasn't a whole lot taller than him and he suddenly became aware of the rise and fall of her chest, of the glow in her eyes.

'I…um…think we ought to discuss this at ground level.'

Something in the way she looked at him changed. She closed her mouth and stared at him. Hard, but without the familiar hint of disapproval. 'OK…Lord Radcliffe.'

When they'd clambered down and found their seats again he said, 'Call me Will.'

She smiled at him. It transformed her face. Without the eyeliner and pink hair she'd be an absolute knockout. 'That wouldn't really be appropriate, would it?'

'It wouldn't?'

She shook her head. 'Barrett told me you're a real stickler for doing the right thing—all that social-etiquette nonsense. It wouldn't do to get too familiar with the hired help. Creates the wrong impression.'

He ran a hand through his hair. 'I'm new to this.'

'I can tell.'

'Is it really that obvious?'

She looked him up and down. 'Your clothes are expensive, all right, but not really suitable for the country. You look like a London city-slicker.'

'Well, I am a… I *do* work in London.'

'Then wear the Armani to the office. Your dry-cleaning bills will be astronomical if you don't get something practical to wear down here.'

He raised an eyebrow. He wouldn't have pegged Josie as being a girl who knew Armani from her elbow.

'The suit makes you look out of place.'

And her clothes didn't? However, it would do no good to mention that now. He was on a mission to build bridges. That piece of news could wait till a later date. For the first time since he'd met her, he couldn't hear the tutting in his brain. And that was seriously good news.

If his instincts were right—and when it came to money and business, they invariably were—she was the only reason this place hadn't closed down by now. She'd be a useful ally and he needed to keep her that way. So he nodded and filed her advice away for future use.

'OK. Thanks.'

The door opened and Hattie skipped in. Josie rose to greet a woman he presumed was another of the village mothers. As they chatted in the doorway of the tearoom, Hattie made a beeline for his table.

'Hello, Will,' she said and plonked herself down on his lap.

Will held his breath.

What on earth was he supposed to do now? He didn't know how to talk to kids, let alone play with them. He looked over to Josie for help, but she was still deep in conversation with the other woman.

He looked at Hattie. She looked back at him.

No smiles. No infantile chatter. Just a look.

A look that said she didn't care who he was or how many grand buildings he'd restored, or even that he owned every stick and stone of Elmhurst Hall. She liked him, and that was that.

Odd.

But nice.

They were still staring at each other when Josie returned, eyebrows raised. He looked up at her, pleading, and saw a hint of a grin flicker across her face.

'Why don't you go and help yourself to a muffin,

poppet? There's a choice of blueberry or lemon and raspberry.'

Hattie was across the room in a flash and Will took no time in untangling himself from the table and chair and getting to his feet. He brushed himself down, although he didn't know why; Hattie didn't have a speck of dirt on her.

'About the renovations. I'll get my architect on to it straight away.'

She didn't say anything, just nodded, and as he left the tearoom he still wasn't sure if she was friend or foe.

Harrington House was visible from a good mile away. Josie's heart sank into her stomach and the car complained as she crunched it into third gear.

'Hooray!' Hattie yelled from the back seat.

If only she could share her daughter's enthusiasm. How Josie could feel claustrophobic in a house with nearly a hundred rooms was a mystery. But she did. Always had.

As they approached it seemed to grow and loom over her. Odd. She never felt that way about Elmhurst Hall. Mind you, it was probably less than half the size of this place and, whereas the hall sat in rolling countryside, framed by trees and old woods, Harrington House was almost the only vertical feature in view, built to dominate its surroundings. Built to intimidate.

She was determined not to let it work on her.

Still, she felt awfully small as she climbed out of the car and pulled the driver's seat forward to let Hattie out of the back.

Hattie ran to the front door, which had opened while Josie had been locking the car, and disappeared inside. Josie pushed the keys into her pocket and walked slowly towards the woman waiting at the threshold.

They both ignored the awkwardness and leaned in for a stiff kiss.

'Hello, Mum. Lovely to see you.'

Her mother looked her up and down, her eyes hovering on the pink bunches. She didn't bother with a reprimand, which was very sensible. It would have done no good.

'You too, Josephine. Your brother is already here.'

She made her mouth curve. 'Great. What time's lunch?'

'We'll be sitting down at one-thirty.'

They started the walk across the gargantuan hallway, the heels of her mother's court shoes giving voice to the tension like the drumbeats of a Hollywood thriller. As they entered the drawing room, Josie's smile approached something close to genuine.

'Congratulations, Alfie!' She ran to her older brother and gave him a squeeze. His sandy hair flopped over his forehead as usual and he wore his trademark silly grin, although it was possibly wider and sillier than normal—almost certainly due to the slender girl standing next to him who was staring at her with unabashed curiosity.

She slapped Alfie on the arm. 'Didn't you warn her about me, big brother?' She gave the girl a kiss on the cheek. 'Nice to meet you, Sophie. Your fiancé should have filled you in on his naughty little sister. Then again, perhaps he thought it wiser to keep me out of the way until you'd said *yes*. Let's see the ring, then.'

Sophie obediently displayed her left hand.

Josie made all the motions of admiring the obscenely large diamond. It was so huge and Sophie was so skinny it was a wonder she wasn't dragging it around on the floor.

Sophie was still staring at her. 'Your hair's... I mean, it's very...'

Her eyes widened even further. She probably hadn't meant to let that slip out, but the poor thing seemed to be in shock, like a startled pheasant from one of her father's shooting parties.

'I think the word you're looking for is *pink*. The name on the box was "Hot-Pants Pink", if I recall rightly.'

'Really, Josephine!'

She turned to face her mother and shrugged. She wasn't apologising for looking as she wanted to look and being who she wanted to be.

Dinner was as long and tortuous as she'd expected it to be. At least Hattie seemed content to demolish two bowls of some fancy apple tart with mountains of ice cream.

Poor Sophie—Josie had only known the girl two hours and she already couldn't think of her without adding the 'poor' in front of her name—was almost too scared to chew. Although she needn't have bothered being so petrified, not with Josie there to suck up all the negative vibes.

Next to Josie, Sophie looked like a perfect angel. And she certainly seemed like one with her quiet demeanour and impeccable manners.

Poor Sophie. If she really knew what she was marrying into she'd run a mile, screaming all the way.

After the meal, when they had retired to the drawing room once again, Josie saw her mother fix a smile to her face and walk over to her.

'Hattie is such a darling, isn't she?'

Here we go, thought Josie. Mother was working up to something, she just knew it.

'Yes, she's a very special girl.'

Her mother's face softened as she watched Hattie, lying on the floor with her head bent over a colouring book, the tip of her tongue poking out as she concentrated.

No doubt her mother approved of the frilly concoction her granddaughter had insisted on wearing. Josie shook her head. Hattie's tights were spotless and unladdered and there wasn't a spot of ice cream down the front of her dress.

Her mother must have been reading her thoughts. 'She looks charming, doesn't she? Quite the little lady. When I remember you at her age…'

Any comparisons were not going to be favourable to Josie. Her mother might as well come straight out and say it: she didn't know how such a disappointment as Josie had produced something so perfect.

Truth was, Josie wasn't quite sure she knew herself. All the seriousness and particular neatness definitely hadn't come from her.

And, as far as she remembered, it hadn't come from Hattie's father either. Miles was the archetypal playboy. Plenty of charm and sophistication with just a hint of danger. And a smile that had been able to melt her knees at twenty paces. She hadn't stood a chance.

And they'd both had too much money and too little sense to behave responsibly. Cue one pregnant eighteen-year-old and two very shocked sets of parents.

'…maybe spend the holidays here?'

She suddenly became aware she'd drifted off and her mother was asking her a question.

'Pardon, Mum?'

There was that look again. 'I was asking whether Hattie should come and spend the summer holidays with us. She could learn to ride.'

'I don't know what our plans are yet.'

She knew she couldn't keep stalling her mother for ever, but a vague answer would give her a bit of breathing room, time to plot and plan.

No way was Hattie going to spend six weeks at Harrington House. Short visits every couple of months were OK, but a month and a half was too long. She'd be brainwashed by the beginning of the autumn term.

All that innocence and joy at discovering life would be lost and replaced by a feeling that, no matter how hard she tried, she just wasn't living up to the standards expected of a Harrington-Jones. Every activity, every decision would be measured by whether it was 'right' or 'appropriate', not by whether it was good for her soul.

Her mother was watching her.

'I know we don't always see eye to eye, but it's no excuse to keep Hattie away from us.'

'That's not it at all.'

Her mother raised an eyebrow.

'You know what it's like in the summer months. I'm going to be so busy with work. It's difficult to plan ahead.'

'How convenient.' Her mother pulled a finger along the mantelpiece to inspect for dust. 'But you don't *have* to work. I've said many a time that you and Hattie could come and live here with us—have your own apartments even, if you wanted a little independence.'

It wouldn't be the same. A different front door would not stop the magnetic pull of her mother's iron will. Before she knew it, she'd be married off to some minor lord who would put up with the skeletons rattling—no, lindy-hopping—in her closet and Hattie would be 'coming out' as a debutante.

'I got myself pregnant, Mum. It should be me who deals with the consequences.'

Her mother brushed the few molecules of dust she'd found off her finger with her thumb. 'Just don't punish Hattie because you don't want to live here.'

'Mum, Hattie is hardly deprived! She's got a lot more than some children have. I'm just letting her have a happy childhood. Not everything I do is a way of getting back at you.'

There was no warmth in her mother's voice as she answered. 'Well, that's a relief to know.'

'I know what you think, Mum. I know I messed up big time in the past, but that's changed. Having Hattie made me grow up and take a good look at my life. I might not wear cardigans and pearls and have married into a good family—'

'You had the chance.'

Well, she'd let her parents think that. Miles had disappeared in a cloud of dust when she'd told him the news. It was less humiliating to let them think she'd turned him down. She *had* turned down the appointment to 'get rid' of the problem at a Harley Street clinic.

'I know you don't understand, Mum, but I want the chance to work life out for myself rather than following some pattern laid out for me from generations past.'

Her mother stopped rearranging the ornaments on the mantel. 'Josephine, the whole point of learning from history—and our family has a rich and successful history—is that it means we don't have to make the same mistakes over and over again.'

She could talk until she was blue in the face and her

mother would never get it. To be a lady, to live in a ghastly heap of stone like this, was all her mother had ever wanted.

'Making my own mistakes, learning my own lessons is what makes me feel alive.'

And she *had* learned from other people's mistakes, just not from her distant ancestors. The generation she had learned most from was right in this room.

She looked over at Hattie, absorbed in her drawing of a princess, and her heart pinched a little.

No way was Hattie going to grow up feeling as if she had to earn every little bit of love that came her way. And while she knew her own teenage years had been pretty wild, all it had been was attention-seeking. Hopefully Hattie would be grounded enough to never feel the need to do some of the things Josie'd done.

She looked over at Hattie, lying on her front and kicking her legs in the air behind her.

It was fine to talk about letting her have her wings when she was this age, more interested in frilly dolls and secret clubs with her best friends, but in a few years' time it would be a whole different kettle of fish. Boys. Drink. Drugs. Avenues for self-destruction would be beckoning to her at every turn.

The urge to keep Hattie at Elmhurst for ever, playing trolls and fairies, was sudden and overpowering. She looked over at her mother again, who was staring into the flames of the fire.

She wanted to lean forward and give her mother a

kiss on the cheek, to say she understood her protective urges but wouldn't be confined by them, but before she'd managed to move her mother broke out of her trance and walked away.

'Hattie? Look out of the window and see who's at the door, will you?' Josie raised her head from where she was kneeling over the bath, ignoring the pink drips plopping onto the bath mat. 'Hattie?'

Silence.

Blast! She turned off the water and dropped the shower head into the tub, then grabbed the carrier bag she'd got when she'd bought the hair dye and fixed it over her hair as she ran down the stairs. Her slippery fingers closed round the door handle. She yanked it open and froze.

Will was standing there, his eyebrows raised and his eyes wide.

Double blast! No one wanted to open the door to their boss with a plastic bag wrapped round their head. Not even if they were the sort of girl who didn't normally care what other people thought about their appearance.

She stared right back at him, issuing him a challenge. *Go on, say something.* The corner of his lip twitched in the beginnings of a smile. He'd better not laugh at her.

She gestured to her hair then reached to catch a drip running down the side of her head. Her fingers were a dark magenta when she pulled them away.

He jerked a thumb over his shoulder. 'It's about the tearoom. I can…come back later if…'

'No! I mean…no. Come in. I'll just…'

She opened the door wide and let him pass. As soon as it was closed again she sprinted upstairs and into the bathroom. He would just have to wait while she sorted her hair out.

Ten minutes later, when the water had finally run from fuchsia through pale pink to transparent, she stood up and rubbed her head vigorously with a towel.

There were no sounds at all coming from the living room as she walked down the stairs. Had he left? The last thing she needed right now was to have to search the estate for him. It was almost Hattie's bedtime.

She flicked a strand of damp hair out of her eye as she entered the room and stopped. Two heads were bent over a game of snakes and ladders. Not a word passed their lips. They rolled the dice, moved their counters, scaled ladders and slid down snakes in complete silence.

It wasn't long before Hattie's counter occupied the winning square. She looked up at Will and they smiled at each other. 'Thanks, Will.'

Josie walked over and ruffled Hattie's hair. 'Come on, princess. Time you got into your PJs and brushed your teeth.'

Hattie smoothed her hair down with the flat of her hand and disappeared upstairs.

Josie turned to face Will and shrugged. 'Sorry about that.'

He looked puzzled.

'Trapped into a game of snakes and ladders. I hope you weren't too bored.'

He shook his head. 'It was fun.'

Fun. Really? Then where had been all the shrieks of joy and cries of despair? He was just being polite.

'What brings you to my doorstep on a Sunday evening, then?'

He picked up a briefcase propped neatly against the leg of the table and removed a manila folder. His fingers were quick and precise, every action clean and efficient.

'My architect has drawn up some plans for the tearoom. I thought you'd like to have a look. If you have any suggestions, please let me know.'

He handed her the file.

Well, there was a turn-up for the books. Somebody actually wanted her opinion on something for a change. All the years she'd spent trying to get Harry to listen to her...

That was the problem with being labelled an *enfant terrible*. Nobody took her seriously. This was her chance to show the world she was more than just a disaster on legs.

Will really seemed to want to do the best for the hall. And, since he had no knowledge of her infamous past, he looked at her without the blinkers—saw the potential instead of the danger. She liked that feeling.

Now, if only she could make sure he *kept* seeing her

in that light. She mustn't do anything stupid to change his opinion of her.

'Do you want a coffee? I could look through these right now if you like. Strike while the iron's hot.' Keep it calm. Keep it professional, that's right.

He nodded and the faint hint of a smile flickered across his face. 'That would be great, thank you.'

'OK…good. If you want to—' she reached forward and cleared a pile of papers off one of the armchairs '—want to take a seat, I'll be back in a second.'

Will looked round the room and headed for a wooden-armed chair.

Her hands flew forward in warning. 'No! Not that one!'

Will was frozen, hovering over the chair, knees slightly bent.

She patted the back of the armchair she'd just cleared. 'Try here. That one would disintegrate under your weight. Only Hattie can get away with sitting on that old thing.'

Will straightened his knees and looked suspiciously at the armchair.

'This one will hold. I promise.'

It only took a couple of strides for Will to cross the room and perch on the edge of the chair. He didn't look convinced.

He also didn't say much. Silence made Josie fidgety.

'Harry let me furnish this place with bits and pieces from the attics when I moved in. Some of it has seen a bit more woodworm than the rest.'

'Oh, I see.' He shuffled back in the seat of the chair, but managed to look just as uncomfortable as he had been when sitting on the edge.

Josie darted into the kitchen and started making the coffee. She had to do something to restrain the urge to babble away like a nutter.

CHAPTER THREE

WHEN SHE RETURNED with two cups of instant coffee he'd managed to slide right back into the armchair. Not daring to risk the other chair herself, she took the folder from him and spread the plans out on the table.

'As you can see, there aren't any huge changes. If we want to get the work done before the tourist season really kicks off, we'll have to move fast.'

She wasn't really used to reading blueprints. It all seemed a bit sterile and hard to imagine. Too flat. No colours. 'What's this section here?'

Will stood up and crossed the room. She pointed at a spot on the drawings and he stood behind her and leant over, following her finger.

'That's the self-service area and tills.'

'They're staying in the same place, then?'

She twisted her neck to look at him and discovered they were almost nose to nose. She hadn't understood why Marianne had gone all weak at the knees at his supposedly 'serious' eyes, but now that they were focused on her she was starting to see where the attraction lay. Her breath stuck in her throat and she couldn't do anything but blink back at him.

'You think they should move somewhere else?'

Quickly, she snapped her head round to look back at the plans. 'Um…'

All the little shapes had gone blurry. She forced her eyes to co-operate.

'At the moment that long, straight layout funnels the customers towards the till. People who only want a hot drink have to queue up behind customers ordering food. I'd always imagined it would be better like this…'

She reached over and picked up Hattie's drawing pad and flicked to a clean page. There weren't any pencils or felt-tips easy to hand, so she used a purple crayon. Will leaned in even closer—she could tell because all of a sudden she could smell his aftershave—as she drew a few ragged lines to indicate the shape of the tearoom.

Then she drew a horseshoe shape with breaks in it.

'If we had separate areas for drinks and hot and cold food—and maybe even two tills—we'd have a better flow of people and it would feel more open and inviting.'

Will picked up the pad and looked at it closely. Then he nodded.

Josie bit her lip.

'I'll get to the architects to amend the plans. We're starting work next week but these sorts of things are finishing touches. It shouldn't hold the work up too much.'

Josie stood up, taking her coffee-cup with her, and retreated to a safe distance. 'Good. Glad to be of help. Any time.'

The urge to babble was getting worse. Now was the time to put the brakes on.

'I'm really excited about the renovations and I've got some great ideas for the styling and decorating. I was thinking of wooden chairs and white walls with large modern art canvases...'

Stop. Stop now!

Her hands had been wildly illustrating her ideas. She dropped them and shoved them in her pockets for safe-keeping. 'Never mind. No need to discuss all that right this very second.'

'OK.' He folded the plans neatly away and dropped them back into the waiting briefcase. 'I'll let you get back to...whatever you were doing.'

Her hand drifted to feel the damp tendrils. 'Doing my roots.'

She fidgeted with the bangles on her wrist as he just stood there and looked at her. He opened his mouth, inhaled then shut it. He turned slightly, looking at the garden gate then focused on her once again.

'What colour was it before?'

What? Oh, her hair! She reached up and touched the place where her hair parted.

'I think it was white-blonde.'

'No, before you started dying it strange—I mean, *different*—colours.'

She made a dismissive gesture, turning the corners of her mouth down. 'Oh, you know. Nothing. Boring. Why do you want to know?'

Will stared over the top of her head. She was pretty

sure he didn't know why he'd asked. He had been a bit talkative for a man who was the dictionary definition of 'the strong and silent type'.

The thump of little feet on the stairs behind her made her turn round. Hattie flew down the narrow cottage stairs and launched herself at Will, encircling his legs with her arms.

'Bye, Will.'

He looked down at the child superglued to his legs and smiled. It was as if something about him had melted and softened. Just for a split-second.

'Bye, Hattie.'

Something like electricity arced between the man and the little girl. Josie could swear she almost saw it. Not a bolt of lightning—more a slow, steady hum— but a strange kind of connection all the same.

All her life she'd wanted that to happen. That bolt from the blue, that sudden realisation that somebody 'got' her. She was still waiting.

It was unfair, that was what it was. And it was juvenile of her to be jealous of his instant rapport with Hattie.

She adored her daughter—really adored her—but if she hadn't seen her arrive into the world and watched the wristband be attached then and there, she'd have thought her little girl had been swapped for another baby. Like those old wives' tales about fairies leaving one of their own in place of a human child.

Mother and daughter were so totally different. And it wasn't as if Hattie was anything like her father, either. She had none of his restless energy or extrovert tendencies.

Will attempted to untangle himself from Hattie.

'Come on, Hattie. Let him go.'

Hattie obligingly dropped her arms and stepped away. See? There was another difference. If it were Josie, and she'd forged that kind of bond with someone at Hattie's age, she'd have had to be prised away, yelling and screaming.

Will faced her again. The smile was gone. He looked about as comfortable as he had sitting in that old armchair.

'Well, Josie. Thanks for your input.'

'No problem.'

He looked down the path again. No doubt he was desperate to escape. Then she remembered something. 'Oh, wait a minute. I've got something for you.'

She ran back into the living room and fished something out of a large bag beside the armchair. When she got back to the front door, she handed it to Will. 'I crocheted this for you. Call it a peace offering.'

He turned it over once or twice. 'What is it?'

Josie tried very hard not to be offended. 'It's a hat. March can still be quite cold in the country.' What else did he think it was? A tea cosy?

'Oh. Thank you. It's very…colourful.'

He folded it in half and put it in his pocket.

'Well, goodbye, then.' And stupidly, as he turned to walk down the path, she added, 'I'll catch you next weekend, if I have any more ideas—if you're down, that is.'

He stopped and looked back over his shoulder. 'The decorators have finished in the private apartments now. I've decided to stay around and keep an eye on things myself for a bit.'

He didn't say anything else, just raised a hand in a half-wave and carried on down the path. Josie responded with an anaemic 'Bye' that lacked enough volume for him to hear, and closed the door.

'Do I have to go to bed right this very second, Mummy?'

Hattie was peeping at her from behind the living-room door. It really was bedtime in five minutes.

'I'll tell you what. Why don't you go and set it up and we'll have one last game of snakes and ladders?'

Hattie didn't whoop or jump up and down, but her smile widened as far as it would go. 'OK.'

As they sat playing for the next twenty minutes Josie stopped herself from shouting 'yippee!' every time she went up a ladder and blowing a raspberry every time she landed on a snake head, and something very strange happened.

Normally, Hattie would frown with concentration and get very upset if she lost, but this time she just seemed to relish the quiet. Every now and then her daughter would look at her and smile and Josie's heart would tumble in love with her strange little changeling of a daughter all over again.

Later, after Hattie had got into bed, Josie read her

a story and tucked her in. Just as she finished reading *Cinderella* Hattie let out a cry.

'What is it, sweetheart?'

Her eyes filled up with tears. 'I've lost Poppy!'

She smoothed the hair away from Hattie's forehead and placed a kiss in the centre of her brow. 'Don't worry. We'll find her. She's got to be here somewhere.'

Hattie never went far without her favourite doll. Thankfully, it was never too hard to find Poppy. She wore neon-pink fairy clothes and had brightly striped legs. The little fairy's outrageous attire had saved her from being lost on more than one occasion.

Josie checked under the duvet and down the side of the bed.

'Why don't you say your prayers while I go and look downstairs?' she told Hattie. 'I'm sure I saw her sitting near the table when you played snakes and ladders with Will.'

Hattie nodded, her bottom lip quivering.

Josie clumped down the stairs, landing on both feet as she jumped off the second-to-last step. It didn't take long to locate Poppy, who was lodged between the side of the dining table and the wall. She took the stairs more slowly going back up, deciding to wait until Hattie had finished her prayers before she delivered the good news.

She stood on the landing, smiling gently as she listened to Hattie ask blessings for each and every member of her class at school.

'God bless Granny and Grandpa,' Hattie continued in a high-pitched whisper. 'God bless my new friend Will. God bless Mummy. God bless…'

Josie held her breath.

'God bless my daddy. I know I'm not supposed to ask for things for myself, God, but could you remind him to come and see me soon? I was really little—only four and a quarter—when he came last time and he promised he'd take me to the zoo.'

Josie ran to the bathroom and furiously dabbed her eyes with a couple of sheets of toilet paper she ripped from the roll. Then she tried to blow her nose without making any noise.

She didn't want to do anything to destroy Hattie's innocent trust in the fact that her father would make good on his promise. The truth was, the last time she'd heard any news about Miles he'd been driving racing cars in Monte Carlo and having as wild a time as they'd had together when they'd been eighteen. She hoped, for her daughter's sake, that one day he'd grow up and realise what he was missing.

But until then, perhaps it was better that his visits were infrequent. He certainly wouldn't be a positive influence in Hattie's life. At the moment, Hattie saw him with the rose-coloured vision of childhood. And in some strange way, that helped. For now, in his absence, he was the fantasy father—funny, charming, devoted. If Miles really became a permanent fixture in Hattie's life, she was going to be awfully disappointed.

Josie held Poppy up so they were staring each other

in the eye. 'We'll just have to fill in the gaps as best we can,' she whispered. Poppy didn't say much in reply, but Josie knew she'd hold up her end of the bargain.

She crept back to Hattie's bedroom and poked Poppy's head round the door. Hattie squealed and when Josie entered the room she found her bouncing up and down on the bed on her knees. She delivered Poppy safe into her daughter's arms.

'She was just playing hide-and-seek. I found her in the living room. Now, no more bouncing. Time to lie down.'

Hattie slid under the covers. Josie tucked the duvet under her chin and kissed her cheek. And, despite the urge to do exactly the opposite, she left her hair unruffled.

Piles of paper were everywhere. A stuffed pheasant sitting on a shelf kept a beady eye on him as he navigated the clutter in Harry Radcliffe's study.

Will had been kidding himself thinking he could carry on with his business and be a part-time lord. Managing this project—no, managing his home— was going to be a full-time job and he needed office space.

The walls were lined with bookshelves and every available gap was filled with boxes, papers and mementoes from Harry's travels. He didn't know where to start.

On a certain level, he wanted to find out more about the man who had inhabited this study before him. Both his father and his grandfather had died when he was quite young and there had been no one to supply answers to the hundred-and-one questions about his family when teenage curiosity had struck.

Funnily enough, he'd never thought of himself as a Radcliffe. He'd been twenty-five before he'd discovered his grandfather had changed his name to Roberts, using one of his profusion of middle names as his surname.

Grandpa had always been very tight-lipped on the matter of family. It was his grandmother who had finally told him the whole sorry tale. Her husband's family had cut him off and pretended he'd never existed. And the only crime he'd committed was to fall in love with the wrong woman. The injustice of it still made Will smart.

Not that his grandfather had ever expressed regret about marrying his grandmother, but it had to have hurt. His family had treated him like an outcast.

Will had been named after his grandfather and he'd been proud of the fact. Grandpa had been the one strong male influence in his life after his father's early death, but he'd been so much more than a substitute parent. He'd been a friend, teacher and mentor.

William Radcliffe had not deserved to die feeling the shame that he'd forever marked his family as rejects and losers. And now Will had the chance to reverse the Roberts family fortunes, to regain the reputation his grandfather had been sure was past resurrection.

The Radcliffe family had allowed Elmhurst Hall to crumble and it would give him great satisfaction to restore it to its former glory, to turn it around and bring in an income to keep it safe for future generations—his children, not theirs. Then they'd see who the failures were.

Of course, he had to find the right woman to have them with. Someone demure but not dull, engaging but not outrageous. Someone who was ready to settle down and have a quiet country life. When he thought about it like that, it seemed an awfully tall order. Where was he going to find such a woman? And even if he did, would he fall in love with her?

No matter. If such a paragon of virtue really existed, he was bound to fall at her feet and worship.

Two hours later, he'd managed to clear most of the desk. It was hard to work out exactly how to categorise the things he'd found. Harry's personal and financial affairs were inextricably combined with the estate business.

It seemed that Harry hadn't thought of running the estate as a separate entity. That would have to change. Maybe he should look into setting up a charitable trust? But first things first. What Elmhurst needed was an administrator, someone to take care of the organisation, the people.

He picked up a photograph in a frame that was sitting on the desk. Until fifteen minutes ago, it had been hidden behind a stack of maps and magazines.

It was a black-and-white and taken, he guessed, some time in the Fifties. A large family group stood on the top lawn overlooking the sunken rose garden, squinting in the sunlight of a summer's day. The man in the centre was Harry. He recognised him from some of the other photographs dotted around the hall. The rest of the group must have been made up of Harry's brother—Will's other great-uncle—and his children. Relations he'd never known.

Since the solicitor had tracked him down he'd had no contact from any of these people. It was as if they didn't want to acknowledge his existence. He put the picture frame back down on the desk. Some of those children would only be in their fifties now. They couldn't all be dead. So much for blood being thicker than water.

Hattie's angelic face appeared at the counter, her chin lifted to see over the top of it. 'Mummy, can I have another cake?'

Josie wiped her hands on her apron and looked at her daughter. 'One is enough, sweetie. I'll be finished in forty-five minutes and then we'll be going home for tea.'

'Please?' Hattie clasped her hands in front of her, looking adorably hopeful.

'Sorry. Why don't you go and sit back down with your colouring book?'

Hattie dropped her hands and her shoulders hunched. 'These tables are wobbly. I keep going wrong.'

Josie put her hands on her hips and looked round the makeshift tea and coffee area they had set up in the corner of the gift shop while the renovations were being completed in the tearoom. It really wasn't ideal. She'd put tablecloths over the assorted garden furniture they'd cobbled together, but it was mismatched and left a lot to be desired.

'Look! Those people over there have finished with the corner table. That one doesn't wobble at all. Why don't I help you move all your crayons and books over?'

A crayon rolled under the table in the moving operation and Josie ducked underneath to rescue it. Just as her fingers closed over it the old-fashioned bell on the door jangled. She backed out carefully, aware that the customers were getting a very good view of her rump.

She began talking as she started to stand. 'Please excuse me. I was just… Oh.'

It wasn't customers. It was the boss. He was clutching a familiar manila folder in his hand. Over the last few weeks he'd dropped by to see her at the end of the day every now and then to update her on the tearoom renovations. Was it her imagination, or were his visits getting more frequent? This was the second time this week and it was only Wednesday.

He thrust the folder in her direction. 'I thought you might like to take a look at these brochures for new tills.'

'That would be lovely, but…' Her gaze drifted to a table of four on the opposite side of the room. 'I just have a few more cream teas to prepare.'

He shrugged. 'No problem. I'll just sit here and keep Hattie company until you're ready. Actually, I've got a surprise for you, princess.'

Hattie's eyes widened. 'Is it chocolate?'

Will laughed and put the folder down on the table. Josie wandered back to the food-preparation area, shaking her head. In between slicing scones and pouring tea she stole glances at the little table in the corner of the room. Will produced a wooden box from his briefcase. Hattie clapped as he opened it up to reveal a chessboard and chess pieces.

How thoughtful of Will. He must have noticed on previous visits that Hattie sometimes got bored on the days she had to fill the space between the end of school and the end of Josie's working day sitting quietly at a table. There was a man who *was* a positive influence on Hattie. She smiled. Her daughter could certainly do with a good male role model.

By the time the last customers crossed the threshold, Hattie knew all the names of the pieces and exactly how they were allowed to move.

Josie took her apron off, hung it over a chair and crossed the room to join them.

'Let's see these brochures, then.'

Will dug the file out of his briefcase once again and handed it over. He nodded towards the board. 'Do you play?'

She shook her head. 'My older brother tried to teach me, but I was hopeless. I was always making illegal moves, sending my pawns whizzing across the board and letting my rook move diagonally.'

Hattie rolled her eyes. 'Mum! It's not that hard to remember.'

Josie laughed. 'I know, but I just couldn't resist

bending the rules a little.' She turned to Will. 'You're shocked. Don't deny it.'

'You're never going to win if you don't play by the rules.'

She placed her elbows on the table and rested her chin in her hands. 'I like playing by my *own* rules.'

Will shook his head and moved a pawn forward one space. 'I'm starting to see that about you. But life follows a similar pattern, doesn't it? If you don't play by the rules, you don't get ahead.'

That simply wasn't true. She knew plenty of people who got ahead just because they had been born with a title or with money. They jumped to the top of the heap just because they could, because they thought it was their right. It had nothing to do with living by the 'rules' and everything to do with the old-boy network.

Perhaps it was just a different set of rules. Whatever. She still didn't want to live by them. She knew her own values; she didn't need anyone else imposing theirs on her. Freedom. Honesty. Unconditional love. Those were the things that were important. She had no problem in living according to those rules, the ones planted in her heart.

The new Lord Radcliffe had a lot to learn if he was still clinging on to the misguided belief that hard work and integrity would get him anywhere in his shark-infested social circle.

It wasn't exactly what she'd imagined. Josie walked slowly through the newly refurbished tearoom, brushing the backs of the sturdy wooden chairs with her fingertips.

'What do you think?' Will looked hopeful.

'It's…' *dull? Stuffy?* '…very traditional.'

'Good. That's the look I was going for.'

Josie sighed as she remembered reams of scribbled plans she'd built up over the years. She'd had such great vision for this place. It would have been fabulous.

Not like this. It was boring. And not just bog-standard boring. It was boring split into two syllables. *Bor-ing.*

'You don't like it.' Will's eyebrows edged a little closer together.

'It's very…appropriate.' She mustn't shudder, really she mustn't, but that word—appropriate. Josie felt a quiver work its way up her body from her toes.

Will's tiny frown developed into the full-blown variety. 'You hate it.'

'It doesn't matter what I think.'

It was his stately home now. He could do whatever he liked with it.

'Of course it does. I wouldn't have asked for your opinion if I didn't want it.'

That was Will all over, she supposed. In the last few weeks, as they'd spent more time together, she'd come to learn that he didn't play games. Unless she counted the twice-weekly sessions when he was teaching Hattie to play chess.

'What's wrong with it, then?'

Josie turned full circle on the rubber heels of her boots, taking the room in.

'All that burgundy drapery looks fine now, while we're only just out of winter. It makes the place look cosy. But in high summer it's going to be a bit dark and gloomy. Not very inviting on a hot day.'

'We're in Kent, not Florida.'

Josie gave him a look. 'I know that. But it can get pretty warm here in July and August. And people get hot walking round the gardens.'

'What would you have done, then?'

OK, she was going to try not to act as if she'd had this memorised for the past two years. 'I'd have made it more contemporary. Light, bright and airy. Clean lines. White muslin curtains. Modern furniture. There's a local artist who was prepared to show his work on the walls.'

'That's hardly in keeping with the history of the place, is it?'

Josie stopped swivelling to and fro on her heels and faced him. 'It used to be the stables. If you're going all out for historical accuracy, you should fill the place with saddles, horses and hay. And where there are horses there's always plenty of horse—'

'OK! I get the picture.'

'Manure. I was going to say manure.' She gave him her best angelic smile.

'Of course you were.'

Will was giving her his trademark deadpan look, but underneath, just for a split-second, she could have sworn she'd seen the promise of a smile. She shouldn't want to see more of that smile. It shouldn't matter to her what he did with his mouth. Even if that bottom lip did look very inviting.

She shook her head. This was her boss and she shouldn't be thinking about him like this. And even if he weren't her boss, she wasn't about to have a fling with another member of the aristocracy. It would end in tears. Hers probably. Hattie's definitely.

Mentally, she added another entry to her unwritten set of rules: ignore Will's bottom lip—and the rest of his finely chiselled face, for that matter. But then her thoughts just drifted lower, to the washboard abs and hard thighs Marianne the librarian had speculated about.

Perhaps she should just try and avoid thinking about him altogether.

While she'd been wrestling with herself, he'd crossed the room and unzipped a large bag balanced on a chair near the door. 'While we are on the subject of new looks for the tearoom…' He pulled something out wrapped in the thin plastic that dry-cleaners used.

She took a few steps closer.

'I thought the staff should have a unified look. Something more appropriate.'

He looked her up and down. Now, this was just a wild guess, but she was pretty sure that ripped jeans and a T-shirt with the name of her favourite rock band on the front was not what he had in mind when he said *appropriate*. Just as well she'd kept her jacket on and he couldn't see the slogan splashed across the back.

He walked to where she was standing, let the

folded bundle drop and she took in the full horror of the situation.

'You have *got* to be kidding me!'

CHAPTER FOUR

'It's just a uniform, Josie.'

'No way! I mean…no way! Look at it!' She held up a hand, keeping it at bay. 'It's grey!'

And knee-length, with buttons right up to her chin and a Peter-Pan collar.

Another one of those shudders started in her boots. And this one registered on the Richter scale.

'I'm not wearing that.'

He looked her straight in the eye. 'All the staff employed in this tearoom will wear the uniform.'

She wasn't so thick she couldn't catch the underlying implication in that last remark. They stared at each other.

This was the point at which she would normally go ballistic, do something completely outrageous. Just to let the person who was trying to squash her into some kind of mould know that it couldn't be done.

'Fine!'

She snatched the ghastly thing from his hands and walked to the door. He followed her and calmly zipped the bag back up. When he'd finished he stood and looked at her.

Don't try it, his expression said.

She clamped her teeth shut. Nobody got away with telling her what to do—who to be. Nobody. But she couldn't unleash the retort she was keeping captive in her clenched jaw. She and Hattie needed food on the table and a roof over their heads.

She glared at him. She was thinking about his bottom lip again. But this time she just wanted to split it.

The door was still halfway open and she swung it wide and marched through it without looking back.

She was backed into a corner on this uniform thing and there was no way around it. And being forced to do things just made her skittish, jittery. Itchy. That was the word. Her mother had always said she was allergic to authority.

As she stomped off down the path she could feel him watching her. Let him. He might have won the battle, but she'd fight tooth and nail before she'd let him win the war. Lady Josephine Harrington-Jones was a one-off, an original. And not even the man who held her future in the palm of his hand was going to change that.

Before she disappeared completely from his line of sight, she slipped off her jacket and let the T-shirt slogan deliver her parting shot: *'The rich must die!'*

Will couldn't help but raise an eyebrow. Loose canon? That was a huge understatement. She was more like a one-woman arsenal.

He shook his head.

It didn't matter. He could handle her.

OK, she was bright and creative and an incredibly quick learner, but she had a wild streak that just didn't suit Elmhurst Hall. This was a dignified place. Any decorating ideas and finishing touches, like uniforms, should pay homage to that.

She rounded the corner into the little courtyard at the back of the hall and he realised he'd been waiting for her to disappear before he moved again. He picked up the holdall and smiled.

She had fire, he'd give her that.

Horse manure, indeed.

He chuckled to himself as he looked around the empty tearoom once more. The sky had darkened from a dirty white to proper grey and clouds the colour of charcoal hung on the horizon. It would rain hard before the end of the afternoon.

He reached over to a panel near the door and deftly hit a row of switches one by one. The lights flickered on. Much better.

He turned them off again.

Hmm.

He wasn't convinced about the funky furniture and modern art, but she might have a point about those curtains.

Customisation. What a beautiful word, thought Josie as the blades of her scissors sliced through the grey fabric. She said it twice more in her head then once out loud, just for good measure. It just rolled off the tongue.

Hattie's head poked up over the top of the picture book she was reading. 'Mum, you're talking to yourself again.'

'Am I?'

'And snorting.'

'I'm sure I wasn't.'

Hattie gave her a look that made her drop the scissors. It had that same shade of disbelief that suited her mother so well. 'Don't look at me like that. It's enough to give me nightmares.'

Hattie merely dropped her eyes and carried on reading.

Denial. That had been another tactic of her mother's. Ignore the troublesome child and perhaps it'll stop or go away. Poor Mum had never worked out it only made her shout even louder or do something twice as bad.

Never would she shut Hattie out like that.

She put down the scissors and crossed the room to Hattie's armchair and planted a kiss on the top of her head. 'Do you want me to read that to you?'

Hattie looked up, a little smile on her face. 'No. I'm OK. I like to look at the pictures for a long time.'

In other words, Josie would only rush her. She tried not to feel the little kick of disappointment as she walked away. Sometimes, bringing up her child to be The Person She Was Created To Be was harder than she'd anticipated.

On her way back to the pile of unpicked and shredded fabric on the dining-room table, Josie stopped to rummage in the dresser. Right at the back of a drawer she found what she was looking for. Pink sequins.

Lord Radcliffe had decreed she should wear the blasted uniform, and wear it she would. But she was going to do it her way.

The tearoom had been open for almost a whole day now. Will had valiantly resisted the urge to hover. Up until now, that was.

He glanced through the glass-panelled door. It was three o'clock and there were more customers than the usual stragglers found here about this time. Half the tables were full with people consuming cream teas as if they were going out of fashion.

If the new surroundings made this much difference, think how much better they'd do when Josie had the new menu up and running. His thoughts drifted to the stack of files sitting on the desk back in Harry's old study.

The tearoom could double its productivity and it still wouldn't make much difference to the debts. If the hall were on an even keel already, it would certainly help, but with money disappearing as though there was a leak in the estate finances, it was time to take more drastic measures.

He picked his mobile out of his pocket and phoned his estate agent. He knew one sure-fire way to raise some cash. His London flat would sell quickly and he should make a decent profit.

When the call was finished, he peered through the glass door again. The only way to get an accurate prediction on how the tearoom had done today was to talk to Josie, but he didn't want to interrupt her if it was still busy.

The door opened and he stood aside to let a large party through. Once they were gone, it was easier to see that things had quietened down and that Josie might have a minute to spare.

He stepped inside and squinted, trying to catch a glimpse of her in the low light. She had definitely been right about those curtains.

Over in the far corner a flash of light caught his eye, something sparkly. And when his brain had registered what he was seeing, his mouth did the only sensible thing it could and dropped open.

What should have been a demure grey dress was…was…

No, it was no good. He couldn't produce any words to describe it. His best shot would be that if someone stuck a punk and a waitress from a 1950s diner in a blender together, this would be the result.

Sequins across her shoulders spelled out the words *Pink Lady*. And where on earth had the skirt gone? There were fishnets. There were legs—really great legs, actually. He tipped his head on one side and took a better look.

Then he mentally slapped himself on the wrist.

This was no time to get distracted. And certainly not by this pink-haired pixie—his employee and the complete polar opposite of the kind of woman he needed by his side to make Elmhurst Hall a success.

She finished pouring a refill of coffee for one of the remaining customers and turned to walk back towards the kitchen. The front of the outfit was just as bad. OK, there was an apron—pink, of course. The silly, frilly kind that was more for decoration than coverage, but there was also…uh-oh…cleavage.

His pulse broke into a trot. He did, however, make a valiant effort to keep his gaze north of her jaw from that point on.

Just as she was about to round the counter she spotted him. She didn't even have the decency to look embarrassed. In fact, she raised an eyebrow and smirked. Actually smirked!

Now his pulse was pounding for an entirely different reason. He hadn't lost his temper with an employee—ever—but he was coming perilously close.

Long steps brought him near to her in a matter of seconds. 'What exactly do you think you're playing at?'

An elderly couple eating a cream tea froze, scones raised halfway to their mouths. Josie glanced nervously at them. He knew he should lower his voice, but he seemed to have lost the volume control. There was something about this woman that made him do crazy things.

She looked back at him and that chin—he'd known

from the day he first met her that that chin spelled trouble—rose an inch.

'I'm wearing my uniform. As instructed.'

'*That* is not the uniform I gave you!'

'Technically, it is. I just made a few improvements.'

A loud snort came out of his mouth and took him completely by surprise.

'The customers like it. It's been a talking point all day.'

He was sure it had been. But not for the right reasons. If they didn't watch out, Elmhurst was going to get a very different reputation from the one he'd envisioned for it.

The elderly couple had managed to take a nibble out of their scones, but were looking clearly uncomfortable. Will grabbed Josie by the elbow and propelled her into the kitchen.

'Hey!'

She yanked her arm out of his grip and rubbed it. The fire boiling in his head must have been showing all over his face, because when she looked back at him she shut her mouth and swallowed.

His voice was low and quiet when it came out. 'I'm going to say something, and I'm only going to say it once, so listen up.'

Josie's eyes widened a fraction of an inch.

'I *never* want to see you wearing this…this…' even now he couldn't find a definition '…again. There are spare uniforms in the locker over there, aren't there?'

She nodded.

'I want you to take *that* off and put a proper one on right now!'

The body language she'd been displaying had, up until that moment, indicated she was crystal-clear about what he was expecting of her, but suddenly there was a spark of fire in her eyes.

'Right now?'

'Yes.'

'This very second?'

Was he not talking English? 'Yes, this very second.'

She kept her eyes locked on his and her fingers wandered to her top button. He was determined not to look down and, for that very reason, it wasn't until she'd started on the third button that he worked out where this was going.

'Not…*right* now!' he said, grabbing the front of her dress and holding the two pieces together.

'Only following orders,' she replied sweetly.

It was at that point that Alice, the part-time waitress, burst through the swing door that led in from the tearoom. She took one look at Will and Josie and backed out again.

Somehow, he became transfixed by the motion of the door as its arc of movement got ever smaller and it came to a rest.

Slowly he became aware of soft warmth under his fingers, the feel of lace. He dropped her dress as if it had stung him and took two very large steps backwards.

'Thank you, Lord Radcliffe.' There was a hard, sarcastic tone in her voice.

'I don't know what kind of game you are playing, but it has got to stop.'

She fumbled with the buttons and did her dress up again. Then her hands went to her hips. 'You waltz in here acting all high and mighty, telling people what to do. It's not on!'

He blew out a breath. 'It's not personal, Josie; you can dress however you like in your own time. I'm thinking of the hall, its reputation.'

'And you think having me around could damage that, do you?'

In a word, yes.

'It could, if you don't learn to be a team player.'

She ran her fingers through her fringe. 'We were doing just fine until you showed up. Elmhurst's reputation is just fine.'

'The place was falling down around your ears and you know it!'

'Well, Harry—'

'Harry's dead, Josie.' Hard words. He hadn't meant to be as blunt as that, but something about this woman just pressed all his buttons at once.

The brown eyes shimmered. A second later a grey trail ran down her face. Her voice was horribly quiet when she answered him. 'I know that.'

'I haven't got a money orchard stashed away somewhere, you know. And all the repairs and renovations don't come cheap. If we don't turn this place around within the next twelve months we might all be homeless.'

'I knew it was bad,' she said in a low voice. 'I didn't know it was as bad as all that.'

He stuffed his hands into the pockets of his new corduroy trousers. Country wear, just as she'd suggested. Now, why couldn't the process flow in both directions?

'We haven't got time to fight about all this.' He nodded towards the apron. And the cleavage, heaven help him. 'If Elmhurst Hall is going to have a future, we are going to have to work together. All of us.'

She nodded. 'I'll get changed right away.'

He leant back against the stainless-steel counter and felt another long breath leave his body. 'Thank you.'

Josie disappeared into the Ladies' with a plastic-wrapped package.

Despite her odd appearance and spitfire tendencies, he liked her. She grabbed life with both hands and lived it. But if she pulled another stunt like this, she would have to go.

A few minutes later, she returned in one of the un-messed-around-with uniforms. It looked hideous. In it, Josie looked grey and flat.

'If you really don't like that uniform, we'll find something else.' Her eyes brightened and she opened her mouth to speak. 'Something suitable,' he quickly added. 'But something we both can live with.'

Compromise. That was what was needed. He was asking it of her and good leaders practised what they preached. He ran his business on those principles and he shouldn't treat this project any differently.

She held out a hand. 'Deal.'

He took it. Her fingers seemed tiny against his as they shook on it. How could something as small and delicate-looking as Josie Harrington-Jones cause so much chaos?

'Deal.'

He let his hand slide from hers slowly.

'So,' he said, gesturing at his checked shirt and trousers with both hands. 'What do you think of *my* wardrobe additions?'

She cocked her head slightly and looked him up and down.

'Will, you look like the country-clothing catalogue threw up on you.'

Her godfather had had two passions: travelling the world and hoarding all the strange and wonderful things he couldn't bear to leave behind when it was time to return home. So, alongside the suits of armour, family crests and the four-poster bed that Anne Boleyn was supposed to have slept in, Harry had filled the hall with these objects of desire.

Every now and then, if visitors looked closely enough, they might find a piece of exotic treasure tucked away in a corner. Elmhurst Hall was filled to the rafters with the stuff. Literally.

Josie made her way up one of the creaky staircases that led to the attics. It was just as well this area of the hall wasn't open to visitors. It was a lawsuit waiting to happen. She picked her way through the attic rooms, dodging model ships and antique bicycles, until she found an elaborate doll's house in the style of a Georgian mansion.

The drawing-room light had fallen off the ceiling again. Josie reached into the Georgian doll's house and picked up the elaborate miniature chandelier between thumb and forefinger, trying not to send a hundred tiny beads flying in all directions.

The hole it fitted in was getting wider and wider. It would probably only be a few more days before it fell out again. But she couldn't leave it. Someone had to care for these things now Harry wasn't here.

The rest of the old toys, musical instruments and assorted booty from his travels weren't in much better shape. She'd done her best patching and repairing the doll's houses, but it was getting to a stage when either they needed attention from someone who knew how to look after such old and delicate things, or they would continue to rot and crumble until there was nothing left.

She let out a long breath and stood up to stare out of a tiny leaded window at the garden. It was a typical April Sunday afternoon, gusty and rainy. Hattie was at a birthday party and, to kill time, she'd gone for a wander and found herself in the attics.

Probably because it was the one place that hadn't changed at all. Everywhere else was familiar and new all at the same time. In a good way. Four months after his arrival, Will's renovations were well underway. The hall was starting to look a lot less derelict.

She could hear precise footsteps echoing up the winding staircase.

'Over here, Will.'

Now his feet were on the bare boards of the attic floor. She turned to find him standing in the doorway, looking at her.

'How did you know it was me?'

She shrugged with one shoulder. 'Just did.' There was something so measured about the way he walked, as if he dared not waste any energy.

'What are *you* doing up here?'

She reached out and touched the curve of an old wooden wind instrument. 'Remembering. Wondering what's going to happen to all of this stuff. It's Harry's legacy.'

Will nodded then frowned. 'What is that, anyway?'

'This?' She grasped the smooth ebony and lifted the instrument up.

'It looks like an oboe or something but...curly.'

Josie fingered one of the brass levers that opened a pad over a hole—similar to those on a clarinet or saxophone. 'It's called a serpent.'

'I can see why.'

She grinned. 'I've been trying for years to get a proper sound out of it.' She put the trumpet-like mouthpiece against her lips and blew. All that came out was a wet hiss.

Will held out a hand. 'May I?'

He took it from her and studied it for a few moments then he pursed his lips like a trumpet-player and blew against the mouthpiece. He was concentrating so hard and looking so competent she was sure he was going to make it sing.

After a split-second a loud raspberry echoed round the eaves.

Will looked so surprised Josie just had to laugh. 'Yeah. That's a much better noise!'

And then he did the most amazing thing: he laughed too. She'd imagined he'd have one of those annoying chuckles that businessmen seemed to cultivate, but the rich, deep sound coming out of his mouth bore no resemblance to that awful haw-hawing at all.

Everything about him seemed to lose its starchiness when he laughed. He put the serpent down and wiped his mouth with the back of his hand.

'Why can I never just have an ordinary, civilised conversation with you?'

She tilted her chin up a notch. 'Because I'm neither ordinary nor civilised.'

He laughed again and shook his head.

There was a tea crate just to her left and she perched on the edge of it.

'Will? I've had an idea. About the hall.'

'Such as?'

'Well, I know that, even with all the tarting up, the tearoom isn't going to bring enough in to keep us all secure in our beds and our jobs.'

'You're very observant.'

He was always so economical with his words. Just like the way he walked: efficient, focused. Even so, neither his words nor his presence lacked impact.

'As much as I love to come up here and wander round in Harry's treasure trove… Well, I suppose it's your treasure trove now.'

He shook his head. 'No. This will always be his.'

If he carried on like that she was in danger of welling up. She'd also be in danger of forgetting he was off-limits. Strictly business. It was never a good idea to get involved with the boss. She took a deep breath and continued.

'It's just that I've been thinking that Harry wouldn't have wanted it to stay up here getting mouldy and gradually falling to dust. We should do something with it. Put the nicer bits up for auction or something. I know there's probably not much worth more than a couple of hundred pounds, but if we haven't got quality, we've got quantity.'

Will leaned against the wall and immediately stood up again and brushed the dust off the sleeve of his denim jacket. Much better than the flat cap and cords she'd caught him in a couple of days ago.

'I've had an idea that I think you're going to like even better.' He paced the floorboards, looking at the assorted objects filling the room.

'I had a valuer up here, looking at some of this stuff, and she reckoned that a lot of it had historical value. The suggestion was to sell the items in collections. For example, to collect all the toys together, all the Oriental chests. And that's what got me thinking. I think we should stage an exhibition.'

Now he really had her attention.

'These old musical instruments could look wonderful displayed together,' he continued. 'We could show all the maritime objects in a room together—the model ships, the sextants, the bells. I find wandering around up here fascinating and I think other people would too.'

This man might seem stuffy and in need of a good tickle most of the time, but he was a lot more perceptive than she'd given him credit for. And a heck of a lot more warm-hearted.

'I think that's a fabulous idea! Harry would have wanted us to fight to save Elmhurst. He loved it here—even if he wasn't very good at looking after it. And he'd have wanted other people to appreciate the things he collected. He loved them for their craftsmanship and originality. No one will get any pleasure from them if they sit up here gathering dust.'

Her voice was husky with unshed tears. 'Harry would have loved this idea.'

She raised her head and locked her eyes on his. There was none of the old disapproval and wariness she had used to see in there in the early days of their acquaintance. Just warmth. And understanding.

She looked around the room. 'There's such a lot here. Where on earth are we going to find room to display all this?'

Will grinned. 'Right here. We'll use the attic rooms,

restore them, strengthen the staircases. People can come up the stairs near the Long Gallery, follow a path through the rooms then down the stairs back near Queen Anne's bedroom.'

That was a fantastic solution. A part of Harry would remain preserved here for ever. Her eyes filled with tears and she was dangerously close to launching herself at Will and giving him a kiss on the cheek.

CHAPTER FIVE

GROOMBRIDGE'S library was always busy on a Friday afternoon after school. Josie pushed open the heavy oak doors and let Hattie run through in front of her. Her daughter ran off to the children's book corner, leaving Josie to return last week's selection.

Marianne was talking in hushed tones to one of the other librarians, as usual. Even though Josie couldn't hear what they were saying, she knew from the intonation of Marianne's voice that *no, really* and *you don't say* made up a large part of the conversation.

As Josie neared the desk, Marianne looked up. Suddenly, both women sat up straight and stopped giggling.

'Coming to get Hattie some new books?' Marianne said in a chirpy voice. Josie just nodded, handed Marianne the books and walked into the main part of the library. She'd inspired enough gossip in the past to know when she'd caught someone red-handed.

There had been plenty of chatter about her when she'd first arrived in the locality. She was sure she must have kept Marianne in titbits for months—a titled, teenage single mother—who wouldn't have been nosy? But living in a small community was what she'd wanted for Hattie. They belonged somewhere, and that felt nice. A few rumours now and then wasn't too high a price to pay. She could handle it.

She found Hattie cross-legged on a beanbag in the far corner of the library.

'Are you OK there, poppet?'

Hattie nodded, while silently mouthing the words to a Dr Seuss book.

She pointed at the adult-fiction section. 'I'm just going over there to choose a book for myself. I won't be long.'

Josie smiled and made her way round the large wooden bookcases to find something fun and light-hearted to read. Her search took her near to the library reception desk and, as she was combing through the paperbacks, she froze, her finger pressed on the spine of a book.

'Go on, Valerie,' Marianne said in a half-whisper. 'What else did you hear?'

There was a slight pause. Josie couldn't see the two women, but she'd bet that Valerie had just leaned in a little closer.

'Only that she's got her eyes on the new owner of Elmhurst Hall.'

Josie felt her spine stiffen. Who had their eyes on Will? He wasn't some piece of meat the local women could auction off to the highest bidder!

'No, really?' Marianne said, predictably.

Valerie made a disgruntled noise. 'Not that he's going to look at *her*. She's hardly lady-of-the-manor material, is she?'

The two of them giggled.

'I heard...' the voices dropped even lower. Josie edged to the end of the bookshelf '...they couldn't keep their hands off each other. Poor Alice found him undressing her in the kitchens!'

'No way!' Marianne hooted. 'Still, she will never be anything more than a fling to him, will she? Not with that awful pink hair and her reputation.'

That was it! There was no way she was going to stand there and listen to this rubbish.

Josie stepped from behind the bookcase, hands on hips. Marianne's mouth dropped open and Valerie started stamping random books in an effort to look busy.

'You know, Marianne, you really ought to check your facts before you start spreading such rumours. There is *nothing* going on between Lord Radcliffe and me, and if there were it wouldn't be any of your business.'

She marched over to the children's book section. 'Come on, Hattie. It's time to go.'

Hattie picked up a pile of books from beside her beanbag. 'Can I take all of these home, Mummy?'

Normally, four books per week was the limit, but today Josie didn't care. She scooped up the books and stomped off to the library desk. What a surprise! Marianne and Valerie were nowhere to be seen. She rang the bell, and one of the other librarians appeared to stamp Hattie's books.

Josie tapped her foot as she waited.

Only a fling! He should be so lucky.

Once she was outside the library's double doors and the fresh air hit, her indignation cooled. Hadn't she just told herself she didn't care what people like that thought? That she could handle any gossip flung in her direction?

Then why did it sting that the whole town considered she wasn't good enough for Will? She didn't want him, anyway. He was too traditional, too stuffy, busy chasing after a life that she had run away from with the determination of an Olympic sprinter.

And even if she were interested, there was no way Will would take a second look at her. He was ruled by his head, not his heart. Any fool could tell that even if there was a glimmer of an attraction he wouldn't be tempted. She'd be bad for business.

And right there was another reason. He's your boss, remember? And the town gossips had already made whole mountain ranges out of a tiny molehill. Think of the talk if something actually *did* happen between them.

'Mummy, you're muttering again.'

Josie blinked and turned to look at Hattie as they walked down the high street together. 'Sorry, sweetie.'

She hadn't realised how attached she'd become to Will in recent weeks. Underneath a slightly crusty surface, he was a good man. Kind. Trustworthy. Even fun, sometimes. She respected him and she certainly didn't want to see his good reputation tarnished because of an association with her.

Lord Radcliffe might not realise it, but he'd do well to keep as far away from her as possible. The sharks would eat him alive.

And she knew from experience just how painful the process of being shredded into tiny pieces—by the Press, by her family, by her so-called friends—could be. She wouldn't wish it on her worst enemy. And she certainly wouldn't wish it on Will.

Later that afternoon, when Will arrived at the tearoom to give Hattie her chess lesson, it was unusually quiet. The only two occupants were Hattie and Josie. They had their heads bent over a brightly coloured book and Hattie was reading out loud in a stilted voice. He was almost at their table when they looked up in unison.

Josie immediately jumped to her feet. He smiled at her and then looked down at Hattie. 'Ready for your next lesson?'

Hattie nodded vigorously. 'Do you think I'll beat you this time?'

He pulled the wooden box containing the chessboard out of his briefcase. 'Maybe not this time, but soon.'

Josie backed away, heading for the counter.

'Don't leave on my account,' he said. 'Sit.'

She shook her head. 'I'll get you a cup of tea. You look like you've had a long day.' And with that she scuttled behind the counter and didn't reappear for another ten minutes.

She worked hard. Too hard, sometimes. He couldn't remember her taking a day off in the few months he'd been living at Elmhurst. He unfolded the board and placed it exactly in the middle of the table. He'd been so wrong about her. Now he'd got to know her, his first impressions had been blown to smithereens. Josie wasn't reckless or irresponsible; she was hard-working, reliable and dedicated to her daughter.

He still didn't understand why she went out of her way to defy that impression. Why did she present this loud, brash front when underneath there was so much more? It was almost as if she hid beneath the outrageous exterior. What was she afraid of? He wondered if all the bluster and in-your-face attitude was just a form of defence.

What had made her that way? He knew very little of her background; she always shied away from the subject. Reading between the lines, he guessed she'd had as tough a time as he had, worse probably. He'd only had himself to worry about, his own worth to prove. She'd been a pregnant teenager—alone—with a brand-new life to worry about.

Despite their very different appearances, he sensed they had a common bond. They were both misfits, trying to prove themselves in a world that seemed supremely unimpressed unless you had class or fame or money.

'Your move, Will!'

He was knocked out of his mental wanderings by Hattie, who had set up the board and was waiting for him to slide a pawn onto a new square. He picked a piece—the first one his fingers fell on—and moved it forward.

He could see it now. Both he and Josie wanted acceptance; they just attacked the same problem from completely different angles. Whereas he was trying to erase the shame of previous generations by conforming to society's rules, Josie challenged the world to accept her as she was, refusing to be shaped by anybody else's expectations.

He almost envied her that freedom. But now, more than ever, he needed to play by the rules. He couldn't choose the path she had taken.

Josie appeared with a cup of tea and bustled away again. It must be really messy behind that counter, because it was taking her an awfully long time to clean it this afternoon.

He watched her work in between quick glances at the chessboard when he moved pieces. She was definitely an asset to the hall. No, more than that. She was an ally.

When they'd finished, Hattie insisted on clearing the game away, her neat little fingers carefully lining up the pieces inside the box.

'Can we play again tomorrow?'

Will shook his head. 'I've got to go out tomorrow. A fact-finding mission.'

Hang on. Maybe he could kill two birds with one stone.

'Josie?' Where was she?

The kitchen door swung open but only her head

appeared. The rest of her stayed in the other room. She raised her eyebrows.

'Could I have a minute?'

She hesitated then walked over and sat down next to Hattie. 'Problems?'

'Yes and no. I'm going to Wilmington Manor tomorrow—scoping out the competition, so to speak. I've heard they have a really healthy turnover and I wanted to see what they were doing right. They seem to attract a lot of families, which is good for business.'

'The safari park sure helps.' She sat back in her chair and folded her arms across her chest. 'You're not thinking of releasing lions in the woods, are you?'

He laughed. 'No. I just wanted to know if you and Hattie would like to come with me.'

'To the safari park?'

Hattie began to bounce in her chair. 'Have they got polar bears?'

He shook his head. 'I don't think so, but they've got lots of other animals—lions and tigers and zebras. Will they do?'

Now Hattie's chair was in danger of tipping over. Josie thrust out a hand to steady it and looked at him suspiciously.

'Why? Why do you want to take us to the safari park?'

He threw his hands open in a careless gesture. 'What do I know about what's family-friendly and what isn't? I could do with a couple of pairs of expert eyes. How about it?'

He didn't add that Josie deserved a day off as well.

She might see it as charity. But she was sharp and, just for a moment, he thought she might have guessed the unspoken reason for his invitation because he saw a microscopic shake of her head.

'Lions, Mummy! Can we? Please?'

How did Hattie do that with her eyes? They'd grown large and round and she looked as cute as a puppy. Will saw Josie's resistance melt. She was a good mother, putting her daughter's happiness before her own pride.

'I'll pick you up tomorrow morning at nine,' he said, packing the chessboard back into his briefcase and standing up.

Josie rested her cheek against the cool glass of the car window and shut her eyes. She let the long rays of the afternoon sun warm her cheeks as Will drove them home from their day out. It had been a long day, draining—and not just because they seemed to have walked for miles.

She'd told herself she would go to Wilmington Manor to take notes, do a job. Anything to help Elmhurst Hall. Hah! The notebook she'd brought with her was lying at the bottom of her bag, only a few scribbled sentences on one page.

She opened her eyes and reached down by her feet to rummage in her large canvas bag. The pad she'd been thinking about was buried under sunscreen, packets of wipes for dirty fingers, a fluffy lion from the gift shop and half a chocolate muffin wrapped in a paper serviette.

She pulled it out and smoothed down the crumpled top page. Only one of the three sentences was legible, anyway.

She sighed. During the course of the day she'd tried really hard to keep her distance from Will, but it had been incredibly hard to maintain professional reserve with Hattie clambering all over him and asking for piggybacks and shoulder rides when they'd walked round the gardens.

Hattie had been so excited to see the animals in the safari park. Her enthusiasm had been infectious. Every half an hour Josie had reminded herself to take a step back, not to fall into thinking they were a family like all the others visiting Wilmington Manor.

And that thought made her lonelier than any other she'd had for years. It *would* be nice to have a partner, someone to share things with. In the past, if she'd dared to dream of finding someone to love both her and Hattie, the man in her fantasies had been a fuzzy, shadowy figure. One day in a safari park and he was starting to look an awful lot like Will.

Never going to happen. Get over it.

He was doing his utmost to buy into the life she was running away from. They were people going in totally opposite directions. Professionally they might work as a team, but personally it would be a mess.

She must have nodded off, because the next thing she knew Will was tapping her lightly on the shoulder and she was peeling her face off the passenger window.

'We're home,' he said in a low whisper.

She sat up straight in her seat and looked around. Sure enough, they were parked in the courtyard at the back of Elmhurst Hall. How embarrassing to have fallen asleep. Well, at least she hadn't dribbled.

'I don't know what to say.' She turned to Will, who was undoing his seat belt. 'Thank you. Hattie had a wonderful time.'

He fiddled with some dials on the dashboard and looked a bit embarrassed. 'No problem. I got some good ideas.'

It seemed natural to want to give him a hug, or kiss him on the cheek, but either of those actions could be misconstrued. She didn't want him getting the wrong idea. Heck, she didn't want herself getting the wrong idea. So she said her goodbyes and bundled Hattie out of the car and they wandered down the path to the cottage.

The sun was setting now and Hattie was yawning. Josie gave her a quick supper and packed her off to put her pyjamas on.

It was only later, when she tucked Hattie in and kissed her goodnight, closing the door gently behind her, that she realised what a horrible mistake their day out had been.

Just as she pulled the door closed, she heard Hattie whisper.

'Dear God, I know I asked you ages ago about my daddy taking me to the zoo. Well, he hasn't come yet, but Will took me to the safari park instead. It was really cool. Much better than the zoo. I'm very glad you made lions. Anyway, I was thinking that—just in case my daddy never comes back from France or Africa or wherever he is—that maybe Will could be my daddy instead? Think about it. Yours truly, Hattie.'

Josie leant against the wall and slid down it until her bottom touched the landing carpet.

No, no, no. This was not the way things were supposed to go! Hattie could *not* start thinking of Will as a substitute father. She just couldn't. Their lives were on different tracks. There was no way they could ever have a future together, even if someone as traditional as Will could even be interested in her.

She scrubbed her face with her hands and ran her fingers through her hair. Oh, this was all getting so horribly complicated.

She would just have to back off even further, make excuses as to why the twice-weekly chess lessons couldn't continue.

Hattie couldn't get her hopes up. She'd already lost one father. There was no way Josie would contemplate a relationship where she ran the risk of losing another.

Will found a tiny brass key hidden on the top of one of the bookcases in the study. He blew on it to get rid of the dust.

Had it been put up there on purpose, or merely forgotten?

He placed it on the centre of the desk and sat down

in the chair. It looked old, and it was too small to fit a door or a gate. It looked more like…

Quickly, he stood up and crossed the room to a small bureau and lifted the roll-up top. Inside was a locked drawer that he'd discovered a few weeks ago. He hadn't wanted to damage the desk by prising the drawer open, and so he'd left it, hoping another solution would be found.

The little key slid into the lock with no problem and he gently turned it, making sure he didn't force the lock. The key felt scratchy as it moved—as if it hadn't been used for a very long time—but it turned full circle and he heard a small click.

A little brass handle was fixed on the front of the drawer and he used it to pull it open. Inside was a stack of documents.

He closed his eyes and prayed silently that something in here would be the answer to all of Elmhurst's problems. Some bonds or an insurance policy that had been overlooked. At the very bottom was a sealed envelope.

The paper was old and faded. He would have put it back and left it unopened if he hadn't recognised the name and address written on the front in fountain pen. Carefully, he eased the flap open. A single sheet of writing paper was inside. He unfolded it and smoothed it out.

He *had* found something precious.

Not money. Not treasure. But answers.

Answers that might help him piece a fractured family back together. And hopefully, with healing, would come acceptance.

'You've got cobwebs in your hair, dear.'

Josie ran a hand through her fringe and grimaced. 'Is it all gone?'

Mrs Barrett walked over and picked at the left side of her head. 'Now it is. What have you been up to on your afternoon off?'

Josie walked over to the sink and washed her hands. 'I've been up in the attics, sorting through some of Harry's stuff with Will. We're planning an exhibition. Will thinks it'll be something unusual that would attract more visitors.'

Mrs B's eyebrow twitched upwards. 'Will?'

Josie rolled her eyes. 'Sorry, I forgot. I meant to say "His Royal Lordship and Master of All He Surveys".'

She grinned. Mrs Barrett didn't smile back. 'I suppose it's all right for the likes of you to call him by his first name, being the same rank and all, but where would we be if the rest of us started being as cheeky as you like?'

Free? Independent? Much better off?

Josie shook her head slightly as Mrs Barrett washed her hands and went back to her floured pastry board. There was no use in trying to explain it to Mrs B. She was a relic of a bygone age, happy to stay 'downstairs' and serve those 'upstairs' for no reason other than that they happened to have been born in the right time and the right place.

'I was going to ask if you'd be able to lend me a hand on Saturday evening.'

Josie attempted to pilfer a warm jam tart from the cooling rack and got her hand slapped for her trouble.

'Oh, go on, Mrs B!' The older woman gave her a withering look then handed her a tart anyway. Josie grinned. Sometimes it worked in her favour if everyone just expected her to be cheeky. 'What sort of help do you need?'

'Lord Radcliffe is giving a dinner party and Barrett has put his back out again. He'll be able to take care of the drinks in the drawing room, but he won't be able to do all that bending over serving the food. I'm not as young and nimble as I used to be, so I could do with an extra pair of hands to help fetch and carry.'

Will was having a dinner party? He hadn't said anything to her about it and they'd been working together all afternoon.

But then, they were colleagues, not friends, and she'd done her best over the last week to forget all the silliness and make sure that the man of her dreams was as fuzzy and indistinct as he'd always been.

Will was too nice. How was he to know that a few acts of friendly kindness could stir up a lonely little girl and her single mum so badly? She'd done her best to keep him at arm's length, but he wasn't taking the hint. Not one little bit.

'You want me to wait on him?'

'Would you? I'm not sure I can manage those stairs to the dining room any more. It's been a good fifteen years since we've entertained at Elmhurst.'

The pastry of the jam tart was warm and crumbly as she bit into it. Heaven. She wiped the crumbs away from the corner of her mouth with her fingertips.

'What about Hattie?'

'Alice would be pleased of the extra cash if you asked her to babysit. She's saving up to go and visit her boyfriend at university. Lord Radcliffe has said he will cover the costs.'

She watched the cook rolling out pastry with fingers that were less deft than they'd used to be. She didn't complain about her arthritis much, but that didn't mean it didn't bother her.

'Of course I'll help you.'

She gave Mrs B a quick kiss on the cheek.

'You're a good girl underneath it all,' Mrs Barrett said, an indulgent look in her eyes.

Josie swiped another tart and ran to the other side of the kitchen before she could be apprehended. She put a finger to her lips.

'Shh! People will catch on.'

Will paced about the drawing room. His tie was choking him. He ran a finger inside his collar in an effort to give his neck some air.

His aunt had sounded rather cool on the telephone. You'd think that finding a long-lost relative would be a cause of celebration. Instead, he'd met with undisguised suspicion.

Thankfully, Barrett had been rather helpful with family information.

If his understanding of the Radcliffe family tree was correct, Beatrice Beaufort was Harry's niece, daughter of his youngest brother, Edward. She'd married Sir Jocelyn Beaufort, a well-known MP. Hopefully, she was an intelligent woman who would see the sense in patching up a family feud that had gone on far too long.

The clock chimed and Will straightened. Beatrice and her two sons were due any minute. Sir Jocelyn had been detained on parliamentary business and wouldn't be able to attend.

He walked over to the window and peered down on to the drive. Below him, at ground level, a long, sleek car was pulling to a halt.

He took a deep breath and tried to work out where he should be standing when Barrett showed them into the drawing room. He sat down in one of the two spacious sofas, but after a few seconds rejected the idea. He would only look ungainly as he eased himself from the squashy cushions and stood to greet them. In the end, he decided to stand by the large stone fireplace. It all seemed rather contrived.

The door opened and Barrett ushered three people into the room. Suddenly he was smiling and shaking hands, trying his best to be charming.

Beatrice Beaufort was in her early fifties. Whilst not the most attractive of women, she certainly knew how to exude style and grace. She hadn't just entered the room; she'd swept in, her two sons flanking her.

Will tried desperately to remember all the tips Barrett had given him: whether he should kiss her hand and what the proper form of address was for the wife of a knight.

'Lady Beaufort, how lovely to meet you.' He extended his hand and shook hers firmly but gently. Her smile only just reached her lips.

'William; charmed, I'm sure.'

It didn't pass him by that she deliberately didn't use his title or address him in the correct manner. But informal could be good. It might mean they were ready to accept him as one of their own.

He waited for the invitation to call her Beatrice, but it never came. He turned to his other guests. Piers was the eldest son, in his late twenties, and looked just as Will had expected him to. He had dark floppy hair and a manner that suggested he'd never had to raise much of a sweat to get what he wanted. Will greeted him with a firm handshake and moved on to his younger brother, Stephan, a carbon copy, only two inches shorter and five years younger.

After making the normal polite chit-chat, they moved to the two sofas in front of the fireplace. Beatrice's eyes narrowed just a fraction.

'So, William, tell us a little about yourself.' She gave a short, musical laugh. 'I'm sure your life before Elmhurst was very…interesting.'

CHAPTER SIX

WILL knew he was walking into a minefield, but there was very little he could do about it.

Piers shuffled back in the sofa and made himself comfortable, draping an arm along the back. 'The family solicitor said something about you being a builder. Thank goodness you don't look much like one.' He broke off to chuckle and look at his brother.

'Yes,' said Stephan. 'I always thought builders were permanently covered in brick dust and had their bums hanging out of the back of their trousers.'

Will resisted the urge to close his eyes and wish them away. He was well aware that he was only just coming to grips with the complicated etiquette his new station required, but he was pretty sure that making personal comments about your host was not the proper form.

Sure, his business had been successful enough that he now could afford to wear expensive suits and play a supervisory role, but in the early days, when he'd been an apprentice, he'd probably been that dust-covered builder they were all joking about—although he seriously hoped his backside had stayed put inside his trousers.

'My firm is quite large now and I specialise in high-end building work. My last project was restoring a villa on a private island in the middle of Lake Garda for an Italian duke.'

The snickering stopped. Piers gave him a lopsided grin. 'Well, that must be rather lucrative. Good for you.'

Will gave him the barest of smiles back. 'I get by.'

Beatrice took a sip of the wine and cleared her throat. 'And how are your family?'

The vultures were circling. If Barrett didn't hurry up and announce dinner there wouldn't be much left of him; they'd have picked him to pieces with their sharp little questions, trying to seem interested, but all the time seeking to undermine him.

If this was what extended families were about, he wasn't sure he'd missed anything growing up an only child.

'My mother and my grandmother are both well, thank you.'

'Your grandmother? That would be Ruby, would it?'

Will nodded. Beatrice looked across at Piers and they smiled at each other. 'Is she still…um… working?'

He'd hoped the subject of Nan's former profession wouldn't come up, since she'd been an exotic dancer when his grandfather had met her. The scandal of their relationship and following marriage had split the family in two.

He looked into his glass as he answered. 'She's been retired for a long time now.' Thank goodness.

The room went silent for a while then Piers and Stephan started discussing the Henley regatta and their plans for the summer. Will couldn't have joined in even if he'd wanted to. He'd never been to any of those events.

He stood up and went and sat in a small leather armchair near to Beatrice. She turned and looked at him.

'You seem a very refined young man, William. I'm pleased to see it, considering your roots. But you have to understand that the Radcliffe family has suffered enough scandal in recent years and we've all been very nervous about you.'

She didn't look nervous in the slightest, but he knew what she meant. He was an unknown quantity and they were worried the family's standing would be damaged if he had any of his grandfather's nonconformist tendencies.

Beatrice continued. 'I'm sure you understand that, in your position, you need to be very careful about what you do and the people you associate with.'

'I assure you, Lady Beaufort, I have never been more acutely aware of that fact than I am at this moment.'

She put down her wine glass and went to study a portrait on the wall. Will followed her.

'I'm sure you'll agree, Beatrice—' if she was going to use his first name, he was going to use hers. He decided to appeal to her sense of vanity '—that the rift in this family has gone on long enough. I was hoping that this dinner could be a first step to bridging the gap. It would be sad to see a great family weakened by conflict.'

At that moment Barrett appeared and announced that dinner would be served shortly. Beatrice gave him a long look.

'As I said, William, it's early days. We might just have to see how you shape up as a Radcliffe first. The last thing we want is another scandal dragging the family name through the mud.'

The tearoom uniform would just have to do. The new and improved version was a nicely tailored white blouse and a slim grey skirt. It was classy, even if it wasn't her style. Or her colour.

She checked her reflection in the glazed half of the kitchen door.

The pink hair was hidden under a black wig, the waist-length tresses braided and secured with one of Hattie's hairbands.

She knew from all the lectures she'd overheard her mother giving the servants at home that the 'help' was supposed to be invisible. Mrs B had hinted at the fact that this dinner was important to Will and her pink hair was about as subtle as a Belisha beacon.

'The starter is ready to serve, dear.'

Josie turned to face Mrs Barrett and smiled. 'All systems go.'

She picked up the silver tray with the quail's egg

salads and headed for the dining room. It was only a small flight of stairs, but it twisted and turned and, as she climbed, her heart began to thump and suddenly it became necessary to check the exact location of every step with the toe of her shoe.

It was silly to be nervous. Will's guests would probably not even make eye contact. She planted her feet together and took a deep breath before she continued into the dining room. She could hear a low hum of conversation. No laughter, though. At least there were only three other guests, so it was a fairly intimate party.

As she entered the room she took a quick look at the company.

It was enough to make her want to turn tail and run back down the stairs at full speed. Her ankle wobbled and all four plates slid to one end of the enormous silver tray. The sound caused the guests to glance round and she bowed her head, desperate not to be recognised.

Of all the people Will could invite! Josie's family and the Radcliffe clan had always been chummy. Harry was her godfather, after all.

She reckoned Beatrice would be an even bet against her own mother in a competition for upper-crustiness and slavish adherence to social hierarchy. Her two sons were no better. They thought the world owed them something for being born into a rich and privileged family. They only had jobs because Daddy had pulled strings. Left to rely on their own abilities, they'd be penniless and homeless.

She kept her head as far down as she could while

still looking where she was going and placed the tray on the large, polished sideboard. Even though Barrett couldn't manage to bend over to serve, at least he was here keeping an eye on things. She was glad of his steadying presence.

She served the starters as quickly as she could, walked neatly to the door and scuttled down the stairs into the kitchen.

'Why didn't you tell me it was Beastly Beatrice and her boys upstairs?'

Mrs Barrett didn't even turn around from where she was basting the duck. 'I thought you wouldn't help me if you knew.'

Josie slumped into one of the sturdy wooden chairs. 'For an old and trusted servant, I had no idea you could be so devious.'

A tea towel came flying in her direction. 'Not so much of the *old*, thank you.'

Josie smiled. 'Does Will know that Beatrice was hoping the hall and the title would go to Piers?'

Mrs B shrugged. 'I haven't said anything. It's not my place.'

So Will had no idea. Poor man. When the evening was over, she'd do well to check between his shoulder blades for daggers.

She could remember Beatrice's face at Harry's funeral. She'd been trying to look devastated but, underneath, there had been a definite layer of smugness. She must have gone ballistic when she found out they'd unearthed a nephew she hadn't even known about.

Josie would have given just about anything to have been a fly on the wall at that moment.

Letting Piers loose on Elmhurst Hall would have been a disaster. He seemed very competent in person—full of arrogance and charm—but she'd got to know him when they'd run in the same high-flying crowd in her teenage years and it was all a veneer. Underneath, he was a waste of space.

'Come on, miss. No time for daydreaming. It'll be time for the soup course shortly. Go and get that big tureen from the pantry, will you?'

Josie snapped to attention. 'The one with the gold leaf?'

'That's the one.'

It wasn't long before Josie was carrying the big tureen, much heavier now it was filled with soup, up the stairs to the dining room. This time she was prepared. The wig had a long, thick fringe and she planned to make use of it.

She and Piers hadn't got on that well in the old days—mainly because she'd always slapped his hand away when he'd tried to feel her up—and she didn't think they'd be on friendlier terms today.

She crossed the threshold and dipped her head. Barrett nodded to the sideboard and she put the soup down a split-second before her arms were due to give out. Barrett dished out the soup and handed her a plate.

Things were going fine until the third bowl. As she leaned forward to serve Stephan, her plait swung forward.

She hadn't counted on the fact that the thick braid would be much heavier than wearing the hair loose, when it just tumbled randomly over her shoulders. The weight of the plait falling forwards turned the wig on her head ninety degrees so the fringe was above her left ear and the end of the plait was dangling in Stephan's soup.

She heard the sound of Will coughing as he choked on his wine.

Carefully, and very slowly, she lifted the end of the plait out of the thyme and butterbean soup. It looked like a paintbrush freshly dipped in cream emulsion. Stephan guffawed.

'Well, I never!' Beatrice exclaimed.

She stood up and flicked a glance at Piers on the opposite side of the table. He was sniggering too. And then he stopped. She was *so* busted.

'Oh, my goodness! Look what the cat dragged in!' he said in his silver-spoon drawl. 'It can't be. Jo?'

His brother turned round to get a better look at her then reached a hand towards her. She so badly wanted to bat it away, but she'd bet that slapping the guests wasn't what Will had in mind for tonight. Stephan caught the middle section of the plait and tugged.

The wig, already a little skew-whiff, didn't bother giving much of a fight and slid to the floor with a thump.

The room fell silent.

She looked at Will. He was understandably mortified.

If she dropped to her knees and crawled out of there as fast as she could go, how long would it be before she reached the stairs?

'My, my, Josephine. I knew you had fallen on hard times, but I didn't know you had been reduced to…' Beatrice waved an elegant hand '…this.'

She was just going to have to do what she'd always done when she'd landed herself in a pickle—brazen it out. It had practically become a hobby before she'd had Hattie.

'I haven't been reduced to anything, Lady Beaufort. I'm helping out. It's a favour, that's all.'

Beatrice's laugh was like fingernails on a blackboard. 'How quaint.'

Josie picked up the wig and stole another glance at Will. The rough fibres of the artificial hair scratched her skin as she squeezed it between her fingers. He was frowning. He seemed puzzled.

His eyebrows rose slightly and his eyes asked a question as surely as if he'd spoken it: *Do you know these people?*

She bit her lip and nodded.

Piers was leaning back in his chair and grinning. She knew him well enough to guess he hadn't finished having his fun yet. It would be better if she just got on with her job and disappeared back to the kitchen.

'If you'll excuse me…' She turned and started to walk to the door.

'It seems such a shame not to catch up on your news, Jo. It's been a long time since we've seen you. The hair was purple then, I think.'

Right on cue. Thanks, Piers. He might have lost three jobs in the City and be rubbish with figures, but he had the uncanny knack of saying exactly the thing you least wanted to hear at the precise moment you least wanted it said.

And Beatrice wasn't slow at egging him on either. 'Yes, do sit down, Josephine.'

Josie stopped and turned slowly to face the party. 'Will?'

He gestured towards a space at the huge dining table. His face was unreadable. She wasn't sure whether he really wanted her to stay or whether he'd been backed into a corner.

She looked at the soup-dipped wig she was holding. A gloved hand reached out and took it from her. 'Thank you, Barrett.'

He gave her a meaningful look. *Watch out for yourself*, it said.

Well, at least if she was here to draw their fire, they wouldn't give Will such a hard time. Perhaps her presence would help. She nodded and walked to the seat, combing her wig-flattened hair with her fingers as she went.

They'd slaughter her, she knew it, but she'd do it for him, because he'd put faith in her and because he didn't deserve their contempt. She'd made her mistakes and she was happy to live with the consequences, but Will had never stepped out of line in his whole life. It wasn't fair.

No sooner was she seated than a plate of soup arrived in front of her.

Piers jumped in before she could get the first

spoonful to her mouth. 'Now, when was the last time we met socially, Jo?'

Jo. That name was part of a different life. It belonged to another person.

Piers broke his bread roll open slowly. 'Ah, yes. I remember. It was Amanda Fossington's eighteenth-birthday party, wasn't it?'

Josie tried to stop the heat climbing up her neck and into her cheeks. Ah, yes. Mandy's party. You'd had a little too much vodka in the limo on the way to the Park Lane Hotel.

Piers laughed. It was an ugly, hollow sound. 'Didn't you get arrested that night?'

Will's spoon clattered into his bowl, sending a splodge of soup flying. She kept her eyes on her own bowl and tried to taste a mouthful. It was no good. Her fingers were shaking. She carefully rested the spoon back in the bowl.

She couldn't look at Will.

Back then she'd been a spoiled brat with a huge chip on her shoulder and a gold card to help her pave her own way to destruction.

'You know I did, Piers.'

'Drunk and disorderly, I seem to recall. Kicked the policeman in the shins when he tried to get you into the car. We all thought it was a fabulous hoot.'

It might have been entertaining for the bystanders, but waking up in a police cell with a hangover the size of Ben Nevis and sick in her hair had not been her idea of fun. She'd been thoroughly ashamed of herself.

Not that she'd ever let on to her fast-living friends. To them it had been a badge of honour.

'Well, that was a long time ago.'

Piers let out a smug sigh. 'Of course, the worst bit of the whole incident was that the paparazzi got a shot of you as you fell into the police car with your dress up round your ears.'

Josie closed her eyes. That picture had haunted her for years. It seemed there wasn't a soul in London that week who hadn't known what colour underwear she'd been wearing. Perhaps fluorescent pink-and-black tiger print had been a mistake. It certainly hadn't gone very well with the electric-blue taffeta ballgown.

'What was that nickname the tabloids gave you?'

Josie opened her eyes and stared at Piers, begging him not to go there. He smirked. Stephan pipped him to the post.

'Lady Go-Go!'

Will's voice cut across the hyena laughter coming from the two brothers. 'You're Lady...I mean, you're *her*?'

Great. He'd seen the stories all those years ago. She'd been secretly hoping he'd been out of the country or had only ever read the *Financial Times* or something. Now he knew the truth, their working partnership would crumble and she ached at the thought of it. Having just one person who believed in her had been worth ten times more than her father's vast fortune.

Piers hooted with laughter. 'Lady Josephine Harrington-Jones! You mean you didn't tell him? That's priceless!'

Josie looked at him. She'd thought she could take this and she'd certainly had much worse than this thrown at her before now. So why were her eyes filling up, tears threatening to push their way past her bottom lashes and roll down her face and into her soup?

Her voice was a hoarse croak as she whispered across to him. 'I'm not her, Will. I *was* her.'

The echo of Piers' laugh was still ringing in Will's ears. He couldn't quite take this all in. She'd lied to him. OK, she hadn't exactly lied to him, but she'd led him to believe… No, that wasn't true either. Then why did he feel betrayed? Floored that she hadn't trusted him?

She belonged in this world in a way he didn't, even if she did her best to ignore that fact. She knew these people, knew the rules and standards they lived by. It hadn't mattered that he was a fish out of water when he'd thought he wasn't the only fish flapping around on the shore, gasping for breath.

All of a sudden, he felt very lonely and then very angry at Josie.

Without even trying to, she had hijacked his dinner and completely ruined his chance of a good first impression. She was a one-woman disaster area.

He needed the approval of the extended Radcliffe family. And not just to satisfy his sense of belonging, of being part of a family. There were more practical reasons why he'd invited them to dinner.

He might have Elmhurst Hall and the title, but they had all the connections, the powerful friends, and having them on side could be crucial to the future of the hall. He'd no doubt with a phone call here and there they could make life very difficult for him. That was why he needed to fit in, needed their respect.

The thought made his stomach turn and he pushed his dish away. They'd been gunning for him from the moment they'd walked through the door this evening and then they'd turned on Josie. Back in the ordinary world, he wouldn't want the respect of these kinds of people.

Yes, he was shocked at the night's revelations, and he was livid with Josie, but just because she'd had a wild past it didn't mean she deserved this...this... witch-hunt.

He looked around the table. His guests were eating their soup and looking unbearably smug. Josie was staring at the salt and pepper pots as if they were the most fascinating things she had ever seen.

What he said and did now was crucial. It was obvious from their treatment of Josie...Lady Josephine...whoever she was...that once you lost their approval there was pretty much nothing to be done about it.

Barrett leaned in to collect the dishes and Josie didn't take her eyes off him. What was wrong? He stopped to watch the butler too and saw what she was so concerned about.

Every time the old man bent forward, his face

stayed composed but the muscles on the side of his neck tightened and Will guessed he must be clenching his jaw.

Josie jumped up. 'He's hurt his back. I can't let him do this on his own.'

Will's guests shook their heads then carried on talking amongst themselves. They'd obviously had their fun. He watched in silence as Josie cleared away the soup dishes and carried them back downstairs with amazing dignity.

And now he'd seen Beatrice and her sons in action, he knew exactly the kind of treatment his grandfather must have faced when they'd kicked him out of the family without a penny to his name. The Radcliffes hadn't changed in fifty years; they probably never would. It was high time someone let them know they couldn't get away with it.

Will turned his attention to his guests. 'You were unbelievably rude to Josie just now,' he said rather loudly.

The Beauforts stopped their conversation and stared at him. Beatrice laughed.

'My dear William, you can't be serious. Josephine...she's turned her back on everything—her family, her responsibilities, her position in society. People like her just don't count. You'll learn that soon.'

Will found himself standing. 'I'm afraid that's a lesson I will never learn, and hope I never want to.'

Beatrice took the napkin off her lap, folded it and

placed it on the table. 'It's no good. No matter what title they might pin on you, you will always be a commoner.'

Will felt every muscle in his body tighten. 'In that case, Lady Beaufort, I think I should ask you to leave my table and my house this instant.'

CHAPTER SEVEN

THE suds in the kitchen sink were a greasy, greyish colour. Every last scrap of washing-up was done.

Josie's wrinkled hands bore testament to it. Elmhurst Hall had barely scraped its way into the technological age. It had indoor plumbing, but that was about it. A dishwasher would have been as out of place as a space shuttle in this kitchen.

Mrs B was sitting at the kitchen table with a cup of cocoa. She looked as neat and together as always, but the way she sat and stared for long patches in between sips of her drink betrayed her exhaustion.

If Will was going to entertain on a regular basis, she would need some proper help. Where help might come from, heaven only knew. It was not as if they could put an ad in the local paper for a scullery maid.

She hung out the soggy dishcloth and said her goodbyes to Mrs B, whose eyes were just drifting shut.

Josie walked down the path that led to her stone cottage. It was an odd little building, tucked into the corner of one of the garden walls, as if someone had just built it there as an afterthought. It was cramped and damp and the door never wanted to shut properly in the winter, but she'd been happier here in the last six years than all her time at Harrington House. It was home.

She paused at the garden gate and checked her watch. Since the dinner had been cut short, it was only ten o'clock. Suddenly fresh air and a bit of solitude seemed very appealing. Alice wasn't expecting her until eleven. She removed her hand from the top of the wooden gate and carried on deeper into the garden.

It didn't matter that the moon was only a fine arc dipping in and out of the clouds. She knew the way to her favourite spot in the gardens by the feel of the path beneath her feet and the shrubs and bushes lining it.

As if to test her, the moon disappeared behind a thick puff of grey and left her to her own devices. She held out a hand and followed the yew hedge for a minute or so until she found a gap.

Even without the moonlight she knew she was in the right place. The scent of apple blossom hung in the air like a cloud. Come autumn it would be heavy with the cidery fug of rotting fruit, but now the fragrance in the orchard was cleansing and pure.

Only a few steps to the right was the lichen-covered bench she'd claimed as her own. It didn't matter how many tourists sat on it to eat their picnics in the summer months. It was still hers.

She reached for the bench and sat in the nearest corner. She shuffled her bottom forward, stuck her legs out, raised her head skywards and waited for the moon to grace her with its presence.

Over the next few minutes her eyes adjusted and the blanket of blackness shifted into mottled shapes in shades of dark grey.

Her heart rate slowed and her breathing became deep and even.

A twig snapped in the corner of the orchard. Probably a bird or a rabbit.

Then she heard a voice utter a short, sharp expletive. She sat up, her pulse skipping, all the good work of the last few minutes undone. Since rabbits didn't normally swear, there was only one other option.

'Will?'

She'd recognise the grunt that followed anywhere.

'Where are you?'

There was a sigh then silence. 'Over here.'

She guessed he must be on one of the other benches further along the hedge.

'Are you OK?'

'Only my pride is damaged—and possibly my shin bone.' He sighed again. 'I was OK until the moon went in.'

'Wait there.'

Josie stood and walked carefully to her right in what she hoped was a straight line. She reached out her left hand and felt the reassuring prickle of yew branches. A few more steps and she should be there.

She moved the hand from the hedge to search for the bench and got a fistful of something thick and silky.

'Oops! Sorry!'

She quickly pulled her hand back from exploring what she now realised was his hair. 'Thought you were the bench,' she added, not sure she was making the situation any less uncomfortable by blabbering on. He hadn't looked too pleased at the dinner table this evening.

Will grunted again.

He was hard enough to read in broad daylight. Here in the dark, with no body language or visual clues for help, she was completely lost. She felt around in the damp air again and found the rough wood of the bench's arm.

The last thing she wanted to do was accidentally sit in his lap, so she patted the seat to be doubly sure before she sat down. He was in one corner and she in the other, a good two feet between them, and there was no danger of any more inappropriate touching.

The only sound was the wind stirring the branches of the apple trees. And his breath. She could hear him breathing. Which made her aware of her own breathing, and suddenly she didn't seem able to do it without thinking about it. And the longer she listened, the harder it became to regulate it.

There was only so much silence a girl could take.

'Come here often?' she said, sliding her legs up underneath herself to sit cross-legged.

'How do you do that?'

'Do what?'

She had no idea whether Will was giving her one

of *those* looks, but she felt as if he were. And he sounded horribly distant.

'In any given situation you think of the most appropriate thing to say then come out with exactly the opposite.'

Josie shrugged. 'It's a gift.'

Somehow, even in the dark, she knew he was shaking his head.

'With your upbringing—by the way, thanks for filling me in about that—you should know better.'

'Oh, I know how to behave in polite society. It's just that most of the time I choose not to.' She paused. 'You're cross with me, aren't you?'

Any other person would have batted the question off, made a neutral remark and denied it. Will, as always, told her the truth. 'Yes.'

'It shouldn't matter who my family is or where I grew up.'

He huffed. 'If it doesn't matter, why didn't you tell me?'

Why did he have to make so much sense all of the time? The truth was she had been ashamed of what she'd done in the past and she hadn't wanted Will to think badly of her.

'I am who I am. Take it or leave it. And anyway, what kind of strange inverted snobbery is this? I was fine to work with and chat to and take to safari parks when you thought I was further down the ladder than you, but now you know we're on an equal footing you've got the hump.'

'That's not it at all!' He wasn't doing such a good job of hiding his anger now. 'I thought you were like me.'

'I am like you! Apart from the pink hair, that is. I'm a human being, aren't I? Just.'

There was a gulp, where she was pretty sure Will was trying not to chuckle, and then he gave in and let it out.

'So…you're a Lady.'

'Yes.'

'Which means that your father is…' He left a space. She had no choice but to fill it. Kind of like a multiple-choice question. The answers she wanted to give were: a) too pompous to live, b) only interested in hunting and fishing or c) terribly disappointed in his runaway daughter.

'He's the Earl of Grantleigh.'

Will let out a low whistle.

Now it was Josie's turn to shake her head. 'I've told you, it shouldn't matter who my parents are. They have nothing to do with who I am now. I'm my own person.'

'Josie, nobody could accuse you of being anything else.'

She looked down at her hands. Even though her eyes were now as accustomed as they could be to the dark, her hands were still dark grey shadows in her lap. 'Sorry I ruined your dinner.'

'If I'm angry, it's because you didn't trust me enough not to judge you. You didn't give me the chance to accept the truth about you. You just assumed.'

Yes, she had just assumed, because finding someone who didn't leap to the usual set of conclusions about her was normally a fruitless task.

His voice fizzed with irritation as he continued. 'If I'd known, I'd never have allowed Mrs Barrett to ask you to help serve that dinner. I would never have knowingly put you in that position.'

Now she was just really confused. Was he angry with her, or feeling protective of her?

'How was I supposed to know you'd invited people I know? You didn't make me a party to your plans. Communication is a two-way street, you know. It's not just my fault Beatrice went away with even more ammunition.'

He sighed. 'To be honest, I had a feeling that from the moment they arrived they were determined to dislike me. Fifty years has passed and the family feud is obviously still hot and boiling.'

He deserved to know the truth. 'Until the solicitor hired the genealogist, everyone thought the title was going to go elsewhere.'

Will breathed out. 'Ah. Now I'm starting to understand.'

'The Radcliffe title can be passed on in an unusual manner. It was a condition set down when it was created, hundreds of years ago. If there are no direct male heirs, the title can pass through the female line.'

'But there was a direct male heir. Me. I'm the son of Harry's next-youngest brother.'

'You're forgetting that none of the rest of the Radcliffes knew of your existence. Harry was the oldest brother, then your grandfather, William. All anyone knew about William's son was that he'd died in his early twenties. It was a surprise to find out he'd got married and had a child before that happened. The youngest Radcliffe brother, Edward, died a few years ago too, without producing a male heir. So, the only grandchildren left were his daughters, the eldest being—'

'Beatrice.'

'Exactly.'

'So, Beatrice would have inherited? No wonder she's cheesed off with me.'

'No, it doesn't work that way. A female can't use the title herself, but it can be passed through her. The title would have gone to Piers.'

'I'd lost with them even before I'd started, hadn't I?'

Josie nodded, although she was aware Will couldn't see her. 'There wasn't much you could have done to make them like you right off the bat. They might come around in the end though, if they decide you are the right kind of person.'

'I'm not sure they are *my* kind of people. They were so rude to you, I sent them packing.'

Oh. That wasn't what she'd expected to hear. She'd known the dinner had been aborted, but she'd thought the Beauforts had been the ones to up and leave.

Her voice seemed tiny in her own ears. 'You kicked them out? Because of me?'

'Yes.'

Wow. No one had ever stood up for her like that before. 'But I made a fool of you! Of myself! I stupidly thought it would help if I was there to draw their fire…'

'No, Josie. You were being kind and trying to help out an elderly couple you care very much for. *They* were the ones who behaved badly. You behaved like a lady.'

Behaving like a lady. Now, there was a phrase that was normally guaranteed to get her spitting. Strangely, when Will said it like that she felt warm inside.

When he spoke again, there was something in his voice she'd never heard before. Perhaps she picked up on it because she couldn't be fooled by his tougher-than-Teflon exterior any more. It sounded an awful lot like resignation. 'I suppose Piers would have known how to get this place up and running. He's born to it after all.'

She snorted. 'Don't you believe it. He would have run this place into the ground in less than a decade.'

She twisted to face him, bringing one knee up to rest on the bench between them. Her kneecap felt warm as it made contact with the side of his thigh. 'Anyway, if Piers was born to it, so are you. You're part of the same family.'

'I can't quite think of it that way. Their life is a million miles away from where I grew up in a tiny two-bedroom house in the London suburbs.'

'Well, you're Lord Radlciffe whether they like it or

not. It has nothing to do with how you feel or where you grew up. You don't need them, anyway.'

He shifted again and she dropped her knee and edged a little closer. She didn't know what to say. He always seemed so together, so confident. She'd never have guessed he felt so out of his depth.

She'd simply have to shock him out of his dark mood.

'You'll just have to find a nice girl with a cardigan and pearls to marry you and you'll be all right.'

'What on earth have pearls got to do with it?'

Ah, that sounded much more like the Will she was used to.

'Well, unless you get your skates on, get married and produce an heir, it'll all pass to Piers anyway. Take my advice; I wouldn't bother inviting them over to dinner again. If ever there was a woman capable of putting arsenic in the soup, it's Beatrice.'

He started laughing. And not just a chuckle. This was full-bodied, hold-your-tummy-and-run-out-of-breath laughter.

'What?' The pitch of her voice rose. 'What's so funny?'

That just set him off again.

'What?'

When he finally managed to get a sentence out, he said, 'That stupid wig when it slid round and dipped in the soup. You should have seen your face!'

She really didn't want to remember the events of that evening, let alone laugh at herself. Her lips twitched, despite her best efforts to stop them. They squirmed as she pressed them together. Will started chuckling again and she had no choice but to join him.

'It's not funny, really,' he said. 'I was hoping to make a good impression on them. I never had a big, extended family with cousins and aunts and uncles. I didn't even have any brothers and sisters.'

'That kind of thing is more trouble than it's worth. You're better off alone.'

'Like you are? Is that why you live here and dye your hair and wear grungy clothes?'

'It's my choice, that's all. At least here I'm free.'

She heard the bench creak as he shifted position. 'You're not free.'

She felt the heat rising to her ears. 'I certainly am!'

'No, you're trying so hard to be the opposite of what you think *they* want you to be that it pushes you into doing things to the extreme. That's not freedom. It's rebellion.'

She stood up, unusually aware of the sound of her boots squishing into the mud. 'That's rubbish! That's just what people say when they want me to conform, to live a stale, stuffy, "appropriate" life.'

There was a moment of quiet. When he spoke his voice was irritatingly calm.

'I thought it was redheads that were supposed to have the fiery tempers.'

She sat down again and stared out into the darkness in front of her. There was no point making a dramatic exit in a pitch-black orchard. She'd probably walk into a tree and spoil it.

She thought of the moment when she'd dropped her soupy wig on the floor. Damn him, if he wasn't making her smile by reminding her of that moment.

'Pink is one step down. Think Madras instead of Vindaloo.'

Without realising it, she seemed to have relaxed back into the bench and turned to face him again.

'While we're on the subject, aren't you a little bit old to be dyeing your hair pink?'

'I'm twenty-four. Didn't think there was an age-limit on being an individual, or does it all die away once you hit forty?'

Will snorted. 'How would I know? I'm only thirty-five!'

'Well, aren't you a little bit young to be sounding like my grandfather, then?'

'Point taken. Feel free to have your hair whatever colour you want. Just try and resist the Hallowe'en wigs in future.'

'Don't worry. I will.'

He reached his arms out along the back of the bench. She heard the sound of his coat scraping along the weathered wood. And felt the hairs on the back of her neck tingle.

'I ended up here tonight because I was thinking of Grandpa,' he said. 'He told me how much he'd loved this orchard when he visited here as a child. He loved to climb the trees and scrump the fruit.'

'That sounds a bit outrageous for an ancestor of yours.'

She smiled. She could almost imagine a serious-looking boy with Will's dark hair and piercing blue eyes insisting on handing over his pocket money to pay for the rosy apple he'd stolen.

'You don't know the half of it.'

She turned slightly further to face him, curiosity propelled her forward and she rested a hand on his upper arm still draped along the back of the bench.

'What happened all those years ago? Harry never talked about it.'

Will didn't say anything for a long time. His breathing changed, became deeper, less even. She rubbed his arm with her hand. He must have loved his grandfather very much.

'Grandpa served in World War Two in the RAF. He didn't talk about the details, but everyone said that after the war he was different. Not in a bad way, he just seemed to want to grab life by the throat.'

She knew that feeling well enough, but life had a funny way of grabbing you back and making you pay if you took too much without appreciating it.

Will coughed.

'I couldn't imagine that of my grandfather. He seemed so proper all the time. A true case of the good old British stiff upper lip, if ever I saw one.'

'What did he do?'

She knew all about the best ways to disgrace a family. OK, her parents hadn't disowned her, but they'd insisted she come back into the fold on their terms or not at all. She'd refused and found sanctuary here with Harry. At least they hadn't pretended she didn't exist. She'd been too young and self-absorbed back then to realise how good they'd been under the circumstances.

'He fell in love.' The way Will said it, it sounded like a death sentence.

'That doesn't sound too awful.'

Will gave a short, barking laugh. 'Well, not by your standards.'

'Hey!' She removed her hand from his arm and faced front again.

'What I mean is that it was different back then. The class system was much more rigid. There were some things that just weren't done.'

She balanced the heel of one of her shoes on the toe of the other. 'Even the rich and mighty are allowed to have feelings, to fall in love.'

'Not with a dancer from a rather risqué show in Soho.'

'Ah.'

'Of course, they were prepared to turn a blind eye if he just wanted to sow his wild oats, but Grandpa wasn't that kind of man. He couldn't desert her like that and go on to marry someone else to keep up appearances. He had to go and do the right thing, put a ring on her finger instead. They couldn't forgive him for that and he refused to apologise.'

'I can't believe Harry would have let a feud like this fester for all those years. His own brother! That just wasn't like the Harry I knew.'

'I must admit that it puzzled me too, but a couple

of weeks ago I found an old letter in Harry's study and I think it might have solved the mystery.'

'Really?'

'It was a letter that Harry had written but never sent. A love letter. He'd fallen in love with a girl that he was sure his family would not approve of. In the letter he confessed his love for her, but told her they could never have a future together because of his position. It was heartbreaking. I don't think the woman it was intended for ever knew how he felt.'

'Oh, how horribly sad. I suppose that could explain why Harry never married.' She paused and another idea came to her. 'It might also explain why he spent such a long time away from home travelling. Perhaps he was trying to forget her. Anyway, what has this got to do with all the bad blood in the family?'

Will didn't say anything at first. She heard him shifting uncomfortably on the bench. 'The letter was addressed to a woman named Ruby Coggins—my grandmother.'

'Your grandmother?' she said, her voice full of disbelief. 'This Ruby was your grandmother?'

'Grandpa said her name suited her because she was the most precious thing in his life.'

Josie smiled. 'That's very sweet.'

'They were the oddest couple. He always wore a tie and suit jacket, no matter what the occasion, and she always wore too much cheap gold jewellery and laughed too loudly at his jokes. But when I remember the way they looked at each other…'

Will sighed.

'It certainly helps all the pieces of the jigsaw puzzle fall into place.'

'Two brothers, in love with the same woman. That is always a recipe for trouble. But still…I don't understand why Harry never tried to make contact. It just doesn't seem like him.'

She heard Will breathe out. 'He did. It was just too late. I remember visiting my grandmother one afternoon and finding her in tears over a letter Harry had sent, asking if he could visit. She wrote back and told him he could visit William in Hither Green Cemetery. He died when I was fifteen.'

Josie's stomach suddenly felt cold and hollow. How awful—for Harry and for William and Ruby. All those wasted years! It just made her more sure than ever that she was better off opting out and not letting 'the family' rule her life.

'Maybe that's why Harry never mentioned it. He was probably ashamed and felt really guilty.' She turned her head towards him, even though he couldn't see her face. The best she'd be was a dirty blob in the darkness.

'What a waste. If only Harry had been able to put the past behind him a little sooner. You would have had all those cousins, aunts and uncles you'd wanted. What did your parents say?'

'Not a lot. My mum was the daughter of a local butcher, couldn't understand what all the fuss was about. Dad died seven years before Grandpa did.'

She slid her arm around his shoulder. 'Oh, Will. I'm so sorry.'

'Don't be.' His voice was hard and she felt his spine stiffen. 'It was his own stupid fault. He always had some grand idea he could restore the family fortunes with get-rich-quick schemes.'

'What happened?'

'He lost our house in a game of poker, got drunk and fell into a canal.' He laughed. 'Literally drowned his sorrows.'

Wow! She hadn't expected that kind of dark humour from Will. But then again, she knew what it was like when everyone had labelled you as a foul-up. No matter how hard you tried, how much you grew, past mistakes were always there to haunt you.

Poor Will! She only had her own stupid behaviour to atone for. He was trying to make up for three generations of Robertses being labelled 'losers'. Suddenly the conservative suits, the stuffy manner, the semi-permanent frown all seemed to make sense.

If only he could see that he was fine the way he was. He didn't need anyone else to rubber-stamp his life and tell him he was OK.

Slowly, she reached her arms around his shoulders and gave him a hug. At first he didn't move but after a couple of seconds she felt his hands slide round her waist and come to rest on her back. She rested her head against his shoulder.

Maybe it was the fact that they were in pitch darkness, and the lack of stimuli enhanced her other senses, but every molecule of her body seemed to jump up and lean towards him. He was so warm and she felt so safe.

They stayed that way for ages, out of words and not really caring, and the warmth of someone else to hold became just as much a healing balm to her as it was to him. She let out a contented sigh. He smelled great. All woodsy and spicy and of…man.

It had been such a long time since she'd cuddled up to a member of the opposite sex—she didn't include her brother Alfie's bear hugs—that she'd almost forgotten how nice it could be.

Not that she was going to go around hugging Will from now on. This was a one-off. Just because he'd had a rough night, and she had the feeling he didn't open up like this much. She really ought to let go now. And she would. In a minute.

Only they seemed to be locked together like two giant jigsaw pieces and she wasn't sure how to drag herself away. Even worse, she wasn't sure she wanted to. The warmth he was generating in her was no longer just where his body was making contact with hers. It was deep down, right in her very core. A sweet tingling she really ought to be doing her best to resist.

'So, Lady Josephine…' He was so close that his breath warmed her cheek. 'You never did say how I should address you from now on. What's the proper form? How does it work?'

She closed her eyes. It didn't matter. She couldn't see him in the inky country night anyway. Had this revelation changed their relationship? Up until that point she hadn't realised how much she'd liked butting heads with him. What was she going to do if he went all deferential and polite? It would be awful!

She opened her eyes.

'I call you Will and you call me Josie. That's how it works.'

Just like here in the dark, all the trappings, all the titles and etiquette could melt away and they were equals. Outcasts in a ruthless society.

She didn't see him moving towards her, but she felt the warmth of his lips a split-second before they made contact.

And the strange thing was it didn't seem like complete and utter madness; it just seemed the natural thing to do. Even as she kissed him back, softly, achingly slowly, she knew that if it had been broad daylight this wouldn't be happening. Something about the blossom-scented air and the warmth of another human being on a chilly spring night made it impossible to resist.

She'd already noticed that Will's movements were precise and efficient. What she hadn't counted on was how devastating this could be in a kiss. Less was definitely more. Every move, every touch was in exactly the right place and doing exactly the right thing—or perhaps it was the wrong thing. She wasn't thinking straight enough any more to be sure.

The kiss ended just as naturally and they both drew back. Her eyelids fluttered open. The moon had reappeared and Will's face was highlighted in silver and dark blue. He looked totally shell-shocked.

Her lips curved into the tiniest hint of a smile.

He started to speak, but she placed two fingers on his lips before the first word was formed. And then she rose and walked out of the orchard without looking back.

CHAPTER EIGHT

THE hits just kept on coming, Josie thought as she twiddled the curly wire of her ancient phone around her finger. If last night's madness hadn't been enough, her brother was now in on the plot to make her life as difficult as possible.

'Go on, Josie. It would mean a lot to me.'

'What colour is it?'

'What?'

'The dress, Alfie! What colour is the bridesmaid's dress?'

'Pink.'

Well, at least it would co-ordinate with her hair.

'Ouch!'

Josie pulled the receiver away from her ear at her brother's shout. Pink taffeta. She was the one who ought to be writhing in pain. She didn't *do* pastels.

There was some fumbling and muttering on the other end of the line. 'Sophie's poking me and telling me it's not pink. It's raspberry crush. I can't tell the difference. Looks pink to me.'

'That's because you're a man.'

Even though the dark, dusky pink she was picturing now had to be a huge improvement on the Barbie-pink dress she'd been imagining a few seconds ago, it was guaranteed to clash with Hot-Pants Pink hair. She felt the blunt ends of one of her bunches with her fingertips.

'Please, Josie?' Alfie sounded a tad desperate.

'What's up, big brother?'

He sighed. 'The whole wedding-planning thing is turning into a huge fiasco. At least if you said yes one thing would have gone right this week.'

'Fiasco?'

'Sophie wanted a ballerina-type dress. You know, all that frilly netting stuff at the bottom.' Josie was glad Alfie couldn't see her face. 'Anyway, Mum has railroaded her into choosing one of those long, thin dresses…Will you stop that, Sophie?'

Josie smiled. 'What does Sophie say the dress is, Alf? A sheath?'

'Yes.' Her brother sounded totally dumbfounded. 'How did you know?'

'Because I'm a girl.'

'And matching green dresses for the bridesmaids,' he added.

With her hair, it would make her look like an over-sized tulip. It sounded as if her mother finally had control of the society wedding of the year and she wasn't going to let go of the reins easily. The poor bride and groom needed reinforcements.

'Tell Sophie I'd love to be her bridesmaid.'

'Really?' The relief in his voice was almost tangible.

'Of course. Now, if I know Mum, the wedding dress is not the only thing she's hijacked.'

'She's sort of insisting we have the reception at Harrington House. Sophie wanted it somewhere closer to home. If we have it at Mum and Dad's we'll never get the wedding we want.'

Josie picked up a pen and started doodling on the pad next to the telephone.

'Sophie's family aren't too far from Elmhurst Hall, are they? Only fifteen miles or so.'

'No, but they've got some major building work on this year and it's not due to finish until the end of June. If it runs over schedule—which building works invariably do—it won't be ready for the middle of July and we'll be reduced to squeezing two hundred and fifty guests into the village hall.'

'And I suppose Mum thinks she's got it all sewn up?'

The indistinct scribble on the pad had somehow turned into a devil with fangs and a pitchfork.

Alfie sounded so weary when he answered. 'She says people would pay a fortune to have a wedding in a grand house like theirs and we ought to recognise how lucky we are.'

Josie stopped doodling and stood up straight. 'Alfie, I've just had an idea. Leave it with me for a day or two and I'll get back to you. I might not have a lot of money to splash around, but I just might be able to give you the best wedding present ever.'

* * *

Will twiddled a pencil on his desk. He was waiting for her. Josie. He knew what he had to say and yet, on another level, he was lost for words.

Saturday night he'd been stupid. Reckless. And he didn't do reckless. But something about the dark and her quiet understanding had moved him. For once in his life it felt good not to be alone, to have one person who didn't insist he prove himself to them.

There was a knock at the door. He dropped the pencil.

'Come in.'

Josie stepped in and he was glad he had the large oak desk between them as a barrier. She was wearing her new uniform and the slim grey skirt hugged her thighs and set off the curves of her calf muscles.

Look at him! Lord of the manor and getting all excited about a woman's ankles. It was positively Victorian.

He focused on her hair. But, unfortunately, it didn't seem to set his teeth on edge as it once had. He could see beneath her disguise now.

'Is there a problem, Will?'

Yes!

Her arched eyebrow gave her a disdainful air.

'No,' he said and motioned for her to sit down in the chair opposite him.

Now he knew her better and seemed to be able to penetrate the hard veneer she protected herself with, he sensed a little vulnerability in her. It had been the same two nights ago.

He hadn't thought about kissing her before then,

but if he had he'd have suspected her to be as fiery and fierce as her persona. And she probably could be…

OK. Mind, get back on track.

But when his lips had touched hers she'd seemed so soft, so vulnerable. It had been as surprising as it had been intoxicating.

'You wanted to see me?'

He'd drifted off again. Blast!

She fixed him with her usual intense stare. 'Is this about the other night? Because—'

'No. It has nothing to do with that. The other night was…'

Incredible? Impossible to forget?

A thousand different definitions raced through his brain and none were the words he wanted to get this situation back on track.

'Whatever it was, just remember you started it— before you get the notion to fire me over it!'

Her chin was doing its stubborn thing again.

'Fire you? I don't want to fire you! I want to…' he resisted the phrase *kiss you again* and continued with the one he'd rehearsed '…offer you a promotion.'

The chin relaxed and Josie's jaw dropped.

'Harry's personal finances and the estate were all intermingled when I inherited them. Although this is my home, I still have to look at it as a business. I want to untangle Elmhurst Hall's finances and run it as a separate entity. I've been talking to my legal advisors about making it a charitable trust.'

'That's a fantastic idea! We could accept donations

and apply for lottery funding. Think of the tax we could claim back from the government under the gift-aid scheme!'

He smiled. He was way ahead of her. But the fact that she'd jumped on all these possibilities straight away just made him sure he'd made the right decision.

'The estate would need an administrator. We can't afford many extra staff yet, but this is one position that is vital.'

Her face fell. 'You want me to work with the administrator?'

He shook his head. 'No, I want you to be the administrator.'

She blinked. 'You want to leave *me* in charge of stuff?'

'Yes. I can't think of anyone better qualified. You know the estate inside out and you're bursting with fresh ideas. And, despite your eccentric choice of hair colour, I think you've got a good business head on you.'

The expression on Josie's face was exactly the same as the one Hattie wore when she beat him at snakes and ladders. He grinned back at her then remembered he was supposed to be calm and professional and schooled his features into something less goofy.

'Do I get an office?'

'That would be a sensible idea.'

He'd already earmarked a disused section of the old servants' quarters downstairs. Gone were the days when the hall required umpteen parlour maids, footmen and under-butlers. The servants' hall, where they had traditionally eaten their meals, and some of the surrounding pantries and storerooms could easily be converted into a suite of offices.

Josie was thinking. He could practically see the cogs whirring.

And, of course, there was another reason for having a whole suite of offices. The only other option was that she share his personal study in his quarters. Since Saturday night, he'd found himself a little...distracted...by Josie Harrington-Jones.

OK, offering her a job where they would work more closely together might not seem like the best idea after their evening meeting in the orchard, but it was the only logical choice.

If they were going to save this grand old building they were going to have to focus entirely on the project, especially if the other branch of the Radcliffe family were going to dig their heels in and refuse to see him as anything but an interloper.

He could focus. He was good at focusing.

'Can I decorate it as I like?'

Will swallowed. 'Within reason.' He tried very hard not to picture posters of rock groups and lava lamps. 'Try and steer away from slogans like the one on the back of your favourite T-shirt, huh?'

Josie smiled. Perhaps he shouldn't have said that. Tell Josie to do anything and she was almost guaranteed to do the opposite.

'The uniform will no longer be necessary, of course.'

The sooner she hid those calves away under multi-pocketed, very baggy cargo trousers the better.

'I was just getting used to this.'

He shrugged. 'You can wear what you want. A lot of the work is going to be very hands-on until we can afford more staff. We have the rest of Harry's stuff to sort through to prepare for the exhibition.'

'Two rooms down, five to go.'

He nodded. 'As quick as we can. I have a friend that works at Sotheby's. I'm going to get her down again to give us some advice about who we can get to do some restoration work for us on some of the toys and doll's houses. I'd like to get the exhibition up and running by the end of July. We could certainly do with the extra cash it could generate.'

He wasn't kidding. Even with his flat sold, the profit would only just cover the debts and bills paid so far. What Elmhurst needed was a steadier regular income from visitors. He couldn't just keep pumping money into it year after year.

'About the finances...' Josie looked at him hopefully.

That was one question she hadn't asked up until now, which showed quite clearly where her priorities lay. As long as she didn't feel constricted and suffocated, she was happy.

'You'll have a rise, of course.'

'That wasn't what I meant. I've had an idea about how to get some more money in.'

'Fire away.'

Josie was so excited she was almost bouncing in the

chair. 'I first got the idea yesterday…but I wasn't sure…now I think it could.'

'Josie, you're not making any sense.'

The next sentence was delivered in such a breathless rush he only just recognised it as English.

'You and me…we could…do a wedding, see how it goes. It could give us a wonderful future.'

Uh-oh. This was what you got for kissing your employees in the orchard. He'd known it had been a mistake. But this? This had caught him completely off guard. Josie didn't look like the rushing-into-wedlock type one little bit.

'You mean… Josie, I don't think that's such a good idea.'

When Josie looked puzzled, Will wondered, had he really read her that wrong? Who would want to get married after just one kiss? He wasn't that good a kisser, was he?

'Why not?'

He stared at her. 'Isn't this a little sudden? I mean, I only just…'

She gave him a begging look. 'I know you've only just given me the job, but I think this could really work.'

'You do?'

'Of course.'

She was deadly serious. He had fun with Josie. She was great company. And OK, despite his best efforts not to be, he was attracted to her. But marriage? Seriously?

'Give me a few seconds to mull this over.'

She crossed her arms, leaned back in the chair and waited.

His thoughts wandered back to the blossom-scented orchard of two nights ago. What had she said about him needing a wife and producing an heir? Not that he wasn't flattered she was offering her services. But he couldn't see Josie in that role.

He needed someone who not just knew the rules of high society, but was also willing to play the game. If he got married—and it was still a big 'if'—he would need a peacemaker, someone who could pour oil on troubled waters. That wasn't Josie. Oh, no. She was the type to light a match and watch the oil slick explode.

Of course, her family money might help—he presumed this was part of the reason. And great families down the ages had made marriages of convenience to cement their positions, to increase their status or wealth, but he didn't think it was something he could stretch to.

Money alone would not buy what he wanted. For the sake of his grandfather, he needed respect and a good reputation. With Josie on board they'd have reputation in spades. Just not the kind he wanted.

'I think I'm going to have to say…' How did he say this? He'd never had to turn down an offer of marriage before.

'Please don't say no before I've told you my plans!'

'Plans?' His voice was horribly croaky.

'My brother is getting married in July. If they have the service and reception here, we could use it as a test run.'

'Test run?'

This was getting scarier by the second.

'Will, are you OK? You keep repeating the last word I say.'

He clasped his hands, laid them on the desk in front of him and tried to look normal. 'Fine. Absolutely fine.'

'If Alfie's wedding goes well, we could plan to book more for next year. I've checked the figures. People will pay thousands to get married at a beautiful place like this. It's part of the fantasy, isn't it? In a few years we might be able to get every Saturday through the summer booked. It would boost the income substantially. What do you think?'

Oh. She was talking about *other people* getting married. Weddings. Business. And he'd thought…

He checked his reflection in the blank computer screen to his left. Sometimes, Will, you rate yourself a little too highly.

'OK. Write up a report with some costings and projections.'

She was bouncing in the chair again. 'Thank you.'

'I don't see why we shouldn't consider it. Weddings are a big earner for some of the country-house hotels I've worked on. I don't know why I didn't think of it myself.'

'Well, you have me now. We can work as a team. We'll get this place up and running. I promise you.'

Her enthusiasm was infectious. He and Josie working as a team to save Elmhurst Hall. Now, there was a pairing he could see working. It just wasn't going to work on a personal level. He'd have to make that clear right now.

In fact, there was still a little bit of the speech he'd prepared that he hadn't delivered yet.

'Of course, if you and I are working together we probably shouldn't…you know…'

'Smooch in the orchard?'

For once in his life he was grateful for Josie's ability not just to hit the nail on the head, but also blast it to smithereens.

'Exactly. Blame it on the moonlight. What do you say?'

'About the orchard or the job?'

'The job.' He didn't want to get into the orchard thing. He might say something he'd regret.

She nodded and smiled. 'When do you want me to start?'

'As soon as we can find replacement staff for the tearoom.'

'I'll get right on to it.'

She rose and headed for the door. Just before she slipped outside, she turned. 'Thanks, Will. For the opportunity. I really appreciate it.'

He let the air out of his lungs and began to relax. The hiccup was over. Things were back to normal. Now, if only he could stop looking at her legs…

'About the orchard…' She gave him a cheeky smile and he felt his lungs grab some of that air back. 'Don't you remember? There wasn't any moonlight.'

* * *

Josie grabbed her bag from the kitchen and waved goodbye to Alice, who was busy serving a group of Japanese tourists. Officially, her shift had ended ten minutes ago and now that she'd changed back into cargo trousers and boots, if she didn't hot-foot it through the gardens and down the lane to the village school, she was going to be late.

Luckily, her bag had a long shoulder strap and she slung it across her body, making it easier to run. Everything was going so well until she rounded a corner on the other side of the rose garden and saw a wheelbarrow directly in front of her.

There was no time to stop. If she tried, she would just skid into it. The only option was to jump. Now.

Her front foot sailed into the air and in a slow-motion couple of seconds she remembered what fun it had been to be Hattie's age, when running fast and feeling the wind in your hair was joy enough.

Then it all went wrong. At five feet two, she should have known her legs weren't nearly long enough to clear a wheelbarrow full of hedge clippings. Her back foot caught the edge of the barrow and suddenly two objects were hurtling through the air and rolling on the floor.

Thankfully, the barrow didn't land on top of her. Its contents, however, did.

She scrabbled to her feet and checked her watch as she started running again, the air slicing in her lungs. Ten past three. She didn't have time to limp or feel sorry for herself.

She dodged groups of visitors as she headed for

the main gate. They stopped and turned to stare at the strange, wild-looking woman picking twigs out of her pink hair.

By the time she reached the school gates she was seriously tempted to slump against them. The so-called 'yummy mummies' turned to look at her as she joined their ranks in the playground. She rested her hands on her knees and took a few deep breaths. She didn't care what they thought.

Hattie's teacher appeared and ushered her class out, careful not to let any children race off if she couldn't see their parents. Josie waved at Hattie to get her attention. Her daughter looked up from discussing something sparkly another girl had pulled from her coat pocket and stopped mid-sentence. Her face was a mask of composure as she said goodbye to her friend and walked towards Josie.

'Hi, sweetheart. Have a good day?'

Hattie nodded.

'What did you learn?'

Her daughter shrugged and started to walk towards the gate, keeping her eyes fixed on her patent-leather shoes.

Josie ran her hands through her hair and pulled out two more leaves and a small twig. Then she jogged to catch up with Hattie. She reached down for Hattie's hand and pulled the tiny fingers into her own.

Hattie stopped and looked up at her. 'What happened this time?' she said in a weary voice.

Josie pulled a face. 'Had an argument with a wheelbarrow. It won. I don't look too awful, do I?'

There was the shrug again.

'OK. Fair enough. But it was because I didn't want to be late for you. It's horrible being left in the playground wondering if Mummy's forgotten you again.'

Not that her own mother had ever done the school run herself. In Josie's case, it had always been the nanny she'd waited for outside the school office.

Hattie gave her a weak smile.

'Anyway, I've got some good news. Will…Lord Radcliffe has offered me the job as estate administrator. It means a bit more money and I'm going to get my own office and everything.'

Hattie jumped up and hugged her round her waist. 'Oh, Mummy!'

Josie blinked in surprise and returned the hug. What a wonderful reaction from a five-year-old! Sometimes Hattie seemed far wiser and older than her years.

'Does that mean you'll wear a suit and go to work like Elizabeth's mummy? You'll be like a proper mummy at last.'

Josie went very still. She took her daughter's hand and led her back up the lane and through Elmhurst's gardens until they reached their cottage. Once inside, she fetched Hattie a drink and a snack and allowed her to watch her favourite television programme.

That done, she walked up the stairs slowly and flopped face down onto her bed. She stayed there, breathing in and out and staring at the pattern on the duvet cover until she heard the annoying music that accompanied the cartoon show's credits.

Once again she was covered in dirt and not fit to be seen. Josie tried to brush the dust off off her trousers but ended up rubbing it in even further.

She stood up and looked around the small room that would be her office when she had finished. The old servants' quarters were partly below ground and a row of high windows looked out on to the courtyard. Every now and then she saw a pair of shoes walk past on the cobbles.

The worst of the junk was gone. It hadn't even been interesting junk. She'd hoped to find a treasure trove of old letters and papers from the glory days of the hall. How many geese and hams had been ordered for long-ago Christmases, that kind of thing.

No such luck.

But at least the space was clear now. All it needed was a good hoover and lick of paint and she could move a desk, a computer and shelving in and she'd be good to go.

The early-evening sun glinted through one of the windows and she checked her watch. Mrs B was looking after Hattie—and stuffing her full of leftover lemon drizzle cake from the tearoom, no doubt. She had just enough time to fetch the vacuum cleaner and give it a once-over before it was time to go and take Hattie home to get ready for bed.

'What a difference.'

As she turned round, she found Will in the doorway.

'You've worked really hard.'

She was about to say hi, but the word was enveloped by a rather loud sneeze. Her nose reverberated with tickle-like tremors. She rubbed it with the heel of her hand.

'Must be the dust.'

Will smiled. He looked very relaxed leaning against the door jamb like that. Not like the man who had walked stiffly into the hall all those months ago. And for once he wasn't wearing a dark pair of trousers, but jeans.

'You need some fresh air. Come on.'

He held the door open and motioned for her to pass by him. She sneezed once again—an aftershock—and walked into the corridor. It didn't escape her notice that Will stepped back to give her plenty of room as she crossed the threshold. Always the gentleman. Always the epitome of propriety.

Apart from that night over a week ago in the orchard, of course.

No wonder he was keeping his distance. He probably didn't want her to get the wrong idea. Every movement, every exchange they'd had since that night had been platonic, appropriate and respectful. He couldn't have spelled it out any better if he'd written it in three-foot capitals and hung it as a banner from the turrets of the west wing.

She smiled and shook her head gently.

No, whatever strange chemistry had fizzed between her and Will, it wasn't going anywhere. He'd do well to heed the advice she'd given him the other night and find a quiet, sensible girl with perfect manners and child-bearing hips. That was the sort of woman Will needed.

She looked at her reflection as they passed a long mirror near to the back door and put the brakes on. Will bumped into her and she felt the solid wall of his chest propel her forward.

'What?' He sounded concerned, but she didn't look at him.

'Nothing. It's just… Look at me. I'm a state. I've got dirt on my face and I'm covered in decades-old dust. I'd be better off going to get Hattie and going straight home for a shower.'

'Nonsense.'

'No, really. You don't want to be seen with me in this state. I'm a disgrace.'

Will moved so he could look her in the face.

'You've been working hard and staying late to get a messy job done. Nothing disgraceful about that. Besides, the gates closed fifteen minutes ago. The only people left in the grounds will be stragglers making their way to the car park.'

He was right. He wasn't really putting himself at risk to be seen with her.

'Where are we going?'

He raised his eyebrows and lines appeared in his forehead as he thought for a few moments. 'I'd like you to fill me in on the wedding preparations. But it's too dusty in here. Let's just wander for ten minutes, let the breeze blow some of that dust away.'

The gardens were beautiful at this time in the evening. The sun was low and glinting through the silhouettes of tall, dark trees on the horizon. The early-summer haze had turned the sky a delicate colour of peach cooling to a dusky blue overhead.

She found herself not paying attention to the details of the various parts of the gardens they passed through, just breathing in the atmosphere and letting the balmy evening erode the tense ball that had settled in her stomach a few days ago.

'What's up, Josie?'

CHAPTER NINE

SHE turned to look at Will, realising she'd almost forgotten he was there.

'What makes you think something is up?'

He didn't look at her as they continued their leisurely pace down a gravel path lined with tall yew bushes. 'You haven't said a word. Do you realise how unusual that is for you?'

He had a point there. Will would have no problem not opening his mouth for days at a time if he didn't need to. Hattie was the same. Josie, on the other hand, seemed to need to get a daily quota of words out. It had been fine when she'd been serving in the tearoom. The gift of the gab was practically a requirement of the job.

But if she spent a proportion of the day in a solitary task, as she had today, she often found herself gabbling at speed to the first person she encountered. She was surprised Hattie's ears hadn't dropped off by now from all the constant end-of-the-day chattering.

'So, what's "bugging" you, to use one of your own phrases?'

She stopped and realised they were at the arch in

the yew hedge that led into the orchard. Will noticed it too. Suddenly he looked nervous.

'It isn't because of…because I…?'

She shook her head quickly and laughed a tad too brightly. 'Oh, no! Certainly not. I'd hardly…'

Now she was doing it too—talking in half-sentences and leaving a gaping space where the uncomfortable words were. Something she seemed to have caught from Will. She'd never had a problem finishing her own sentences before he'd come along and…

'No, Will. Don't fret. I've been worrying about Hattie, that's all.'

They both looked again at the hole in the hedge that led to the orchard and, as one, set off in the opposite direction.

'There's nothing wrong, is there? She's not ill or anything?'

Josie shook her head. A bout of chickenpox would have been much easier to deal with. She could read her family-health encyclopaedia and follow the advice, no help required. No, this was a question she simply couldn't answer on her own.

If only she had the kind of family she could talk to. She'd had the oddest ache to phone her mother and ask for advice. But that would do no good. Mum would never understand. She feared the answer she'd get would only confirm that sad little look in Hattie's eyes.

The words burst from her before she'd even had a chance to think about them. 'Do you think I'm a good mother?'

She couldn't look at him. Just in case he'd have the look in his eyes too. The one that said all her efforts had fallen short of the mark once again. He made an uncomfortable noise in the back of his throat and, as she stared at the gravel path, she saw him grind a section of it with the toe of his shoe.

'I don't really know anything about children. I'm hardly qualified to…'

Yep. Just what she'd feared. Somewhere along the line, as she'd been trying to do a heck of a better job than her own mother had, she'd only succeeded in screwing up in a different way. Trust her to find a new way to end up in the same old mess.

She didn't know why she kept talking. She should have cut and run right there before she heard anything else that shredded her sense of self-worth, but she couldn't stop. Just for once she needed someone else.

Odd that the someone else had turned out to be Will, but she supposed he was the closest thing she had to a friend since Harry had died.

'You know what she said the other day, when I told her about the new job?' She didn't wait for him to answer. 'She was really pleased because I would be a "proper" mummy.'

A loud sniff accompanied her next breath.

'All these years I thought I was doing the right thing, raising her to be free to be who she wants to be. I thought I was showing her that it's OK to be herself, OK to be an individual. Turns out she wants me to be like the rest of them. A cookie-cutter mum with neat hair, a Volvo and nothing to talk about but this week's soaps and reality-TV shows.'

'I'm not sure I can see you in a Volvo.'

Another sniff escaped.

'But she can! That's the point. That's what she wants from me and I'm not sure I can give it to her without twisting myself into something I'm not. Either way, one of us is going to be miserable.'

A meticulously folded white handkerchief appeared under her nose. Her *thank you* was muffled as she made use of it. And then a strong hand reached around her, settled on her back and drew her into a T-shirted chest.

How embarrassing.

His voice was quiet and rumbled in her ear. 'One of the things I like most about you is that you don't care what anyone thinks of you. Me, I worry about that all the time. After Grandpa's fall from grace, it became a genetic trait. Sometimes I wish I could just dye my hair pink and tell the world to "stuff it" too.'

Any other time and she'd probably have giggled about the idea of Will with pink hair. She pulled herself away and swiped at her eyes.

'I don't care what the world thinks. I care about what Hattie thinks. And if she thinks I'm a failure, I don't know what I'll do.' She lifted her face and looked at him through tear-blurred eyes. 'I might as well give up, move back home and let my mother run my life again.'

'No.' There was such a firmness in his voice it made her freeze.

She blinked away some of the congealing tears.

'Give her some time, Josie. She's only five. In a few years she'll appreciate what a gift it is to have a mother who wants her to follow her dreams. Don't change yourself.'

There was an odd look in his eyes that made her heart quiver.

'Be who you were born to be. That's what my grandfather always used to say.' He looked back towards the house, its roof and spindly chimneys still in view beyond the hedge. 'That's what I intend to do. This house, reclaiming this family—this is what I was born to do. I didn't know it at first, but now I can't escape it.'

He took a deep breath. 'I'm totally handing over the running of my property-development business to my partner and I'm concentrating all my energies on getting this place on its feet.'

'Will, that's wonderful.' She wiped her nose one last time and looked at the hanky. 'I'll wash this before giving it back to you.'

He laughed. 'I appreciate that.'

They turned back towards the house and fell into step. Somehow, even though his legs seemed twice as long as hers, she never struggled to keep up. How did he do that?

He didn't seem to be walking uncomfortably slowly for his large frame. Somehow, he just adjusted and made it easy for her to fit with him. If only she could learn to fit in with people. It might prove useful in tying together all the different pieces of her life.

But if there was one thing she knew about herself, it was that she was an all-or-nothing kind of gal. With her, it always seemed to be the choice between two extremes. Middle ground might as well be a foreign country.

He smiled at her as they took the short cut through the magnolia garden. 'Now, tell me what weird and wonderful ideas you've been having about this wedding.'

'Yes, Mum. Of course I haven't forgotten to book the string quartet. And no, I haven't switched them for a punk band while your back has been turned.'

Josie drummed the end of her pen on her desk and stared at the exploding fireworks on her screensaver.

For goodness' sake! It was a long time since she'd pulled the same stunt at her sweet-sixteen party. She was a grown woman now. With a child of her own. When was her mother going to realise she was an adult?

She made the right soothing noises to her mother and managed to put the phone down after a drawn-out goodbye sprinkled with snippets of advice. It was the tenth call this week and Mother Dear was slowly driving her insane. She hadn't let go of the reins of the wedding now it had a new venue; she just had a different set of ears to nag.

Poor Sophie, indeed. Poor Sophie was probably sitting at home chortling into her bone-china teaset and congratulating herself on her escape. Alfie was no help at all. Mum just had to look at him and he caved in.

So, while Alfie and Sophie were adamant they

wanted lilies, they wouldn't admit that to Sergeant-Major Mummy and it was down to Josie to explain for the umpteenth time why they weren't having roses.

As a result, Alfie and Sophie, who she was starting to suspect was a lot more cunning than she'd ever given her credit for, were the golden couple and—surprise, surprise—once again, Josie was the troublemaker.

'Are you busy?'

She looked up to see Will hovering in her doorway. No, hovering was the wrong word. Will would never do something as indecisive as hover. He was merely *there*, filling the space and waiting for her to answer.

He'd moved his computer and files into one of the other offices along this corridor. They'd both thought it sensible for her not to have to run up two flights of stairs to the study if she needed to chat to him about something. He was keeping that for personal use.

'Always. You get very good value for money with me, you know.'

'I know.'

Her heart did a silly flutter inside her chest. It was nice to be appreciated, nice to have someone who trusted her and didn't expect to bail her out every two minutes.

'I've got something to show you.'

She cleared a space on her desk in preparation.

'No, out here. I'm going to have to shoe-horn you out of your office for ten minutes.'

She rose and slid her feet into her sandals. May had been hot and sunny so far and the visitors had flocked to Elmhurst in record numbers. And, if preliminary figures were anything to go by, they were staying longer and spending more money on food and souvenirs when they got here.

'I've found something truly spectacular up in the attic. I think you need to come and see.'

She picked up speed as they navigated the warren of corridors in this section of the house and headed up the back stairs. He always stayed just a few feet behind her, close enough so she could feel his presence, but never close enough to touch.

When they reached the top of the attic stairs she stopped and let him pass her. 'Which way?'

He pointed to one of the small rooms on the left.

The job of sorting through Harry's collection had been long, dusty and complicated. Add to that the fact that they only managed to find a few snatched hours each week and it seemed as if it would take for ever. Only last night they'd finished going through the penultimate room and it seemed Will hadn't been able to resist a peek today when he should have been having his lunch break.

The narrow corridor was lined with carvings and exotic masks and they had to turn sideways on occasion to squeeze through the gaps between ornate oriental chests. Will had had the idea of sorting everything into piles of the same kind. It was just the way his neat and ordered mind seemed to work.

Now, as Josie peeked in the doorways they passed, she realised what a good idea it had been. One old wooden bicycle was interesting, but seeing twenty together, all slightly different shapes and sizes, was fascinating. She could almost guess at the chronological order by looking at the styles of saddles and wheels.

Will stopped in the doorway of the farthest—and by far the dirtiest and most cluttered room—in the attic. It was so crammed full of stuff, they hadn't known where to start. Hence the decision to leave it till last.

'Wait there.'

Josie stood at the threshold as Will disappeared into the room. She waited a few moments, hearing scuffling from somewhere inside. Then it all went quiet. What was he doing in there? Was he all right?

She poked her head round the corner then leapt back, almost toppling over a box of assorted china as something large and fierce-looking pounced at her.

The sound of Will's low, reverberating chuckle filled the air.

She shook her head, trying to dislodge the sound of her runaway heart in her ears. Will was standing in front of her with some kind of helmet on—complete with nose, grimacing mouth and a moustache made from bristles. Gold antlers balanced on top. He undid the chin strap and pulled it off.

'What the heck do you think you are doing?'

'It's a suit of Japanese armour. Pretty spectacular, huh? I thought you should get the full effect.'

'Of all the…' She was too boiling mad to finish that sentence. What she wanted to say would only get her fired.

He looked at her solemnly and nodded. 'Ah, I see.'

'See what?' she snapped.

'You can dish it out, but you can't take it.'

She folded her arms across her chest. 'What is that supposed to mean? Will, you are in a seriously strange mood today.'

'It means, Lady Harrington-Jones, that you are as happy as Larry when you are the one dishing out the shocks, but you don't like it one little bit when the tables are turned.'

'Oh, so that's what it was. A lesson in self-awareness. Thank you so much.'

Will rested the helmet on top of a large wooden crate. It seemed to be grinning at her with that empty black mouth full of metal teeth.

'I thought you would appreciate the joke, that's all. Lighten up. You've become all serious over the last few weeks.'

She pre-empted a smile by pursing her lips. 'It's working for you, you big nut. It's very stressful.'

'So I've heard.' It didn't seem to bother him at all. In fact, he was still grinning. 'Josie, there is a complete suit of armour in an old wardrobe over there. It's spectacular! And what's more, it's probably worth thousands. We should display it with the samurai swords and Japanese chests. It should be a real draw.'

She picked up a dirty rag that was sitting near by and threw it at him. 'Just don't pull any stunts like that again, you hear?'

Will at least *tried* to look repentant.

She looked at the mask of the helmet sitting a few feet away, face frozen in perpetual anger, then she looked Will straight in the eyes. 'And take that hideous mask off at once. You're starting to scare me.'

There was no other way to describe it. Josie was blossoming, Will thought as he watched her on the telephone. Of course, he'd had faith in her when he'd offered her this job, but even he hadn't bargained for the transformation that would take place.

Oh, the hair was still pink. Luminous pink. But other little changes were starting to snowball. While she hadn't abandoned her normal style for a business-suited look, the subtle changes were much more appropriate.

The make-up had toned down and today she wore a floaty summer skirt printed with magnolias. And pretty flip-flops studded with jewels. He'd noticed because, despite his best efforts to rid himself of it, his fixation with her ankles hadn't abated, and it wasn't helped by the delicate Indian chain she wore on one foot. It jingled gently as she walked and drew his gaze like a magnet.

But more than the clothes, it was the confidence she exuded, the life shining out of her now she'd jumped in wholeheartedly to the difficult job of getting this estate streamlined and efficient. She was succeeding.

And rather than being a loose canon, she seemed to know how to handle each and every catastrophe. She was charming rather than loud and outspoken, although she knew how to be pushy when she needed to be.

He was completely in awe of the way she'd handled this wedding, which seemed to be growing out of all proportion into the social spectacular of the decade. He wouldn't have been surprised if her mother had requested Elmhurst Hall be picked up and moved twenty feet to the right, just to give the marquee a little more room.

The whole rigmarole was starting to put him off the idea of ever getting hitched. At least that was the reason he gave himself for not being out enjoying the summer season and hunting for an appropriate woman to bear him heirs.

Josie put down the phone and frowned.

'Don't tell me, your mother has decided we're abandoning the Madeira cake and going back to fruit cake again.'

She rested her elbows on her desk and ran her fingers through her hair. It made her pink fringe stick up in the most adorable way.

'It's worse. The photographer has cancelled.'

He instantly shot to his feet. 'What? We've only got three weeks to go.'

'Don't ask me how, but I can smell Beaufort interference all over this.'

'Really? You don't think they'd stoop so low, do you?'

She raised her eyebrows and gave him a look. 'I think they'd do anything they fancied if they thought it would keep you in your place.'

He sat back down in the chair opposite her desk. He'd had a question about the new information brochure they were working on, but that could wait. She grimaced and rubbed her jaw.

'They must have realised this wedding business could be a big money-spinner and they want to put a stop to it.'

'But why? They don't have to like me, but why would they go out of their way to sabotage the family like this?'

She gave him a glum look. 'I'm sorry to say, Will, that they don't see you as family; they see you as competition. And even if they can't get their hands on Elmhurst, they'd like to be proved right that you didn't deserve it in the first place. It makes them feel superior.'

'This whole having a family thing is a lot more complicated than I'd imagined.'

She tipped her head to one side and smiled at him. The wayward bit of fringe dropped back into place. 'Not all big families are like that.' She frowned. 'Don't know why I'm sounding so positive. Mine are almost as bad.'

'At least your mother isn't trying to make sure all your efforts come to nothing.'

She raised her eyebrows. 'Oh, yeah? Then what's all this shilly-shallying about the stupid cake, then? She's trying to drive me insane… Ouch!'

She rubbed the side of her face again. That was the second time this morning. Come to think of it, he'd seen her do it a couple of times in the last few days as well.

'What's wrong?'

She carried on rubbing. 'Nothing. Really.'

'It's your teeth, isn't it?'

'Don't worry, Will. It's just a twinge. It'll sort itself out. And if it doesn't, I'll go to the dentist after the wedding is over.' A long sigh followed. 'Suppose I'd better start ringing round to find a replacement photographer. Although it's not going to be easy. Whoever heard of a good—no, fabulous—wedding photographer who has a hole in his schedule at this time of year?'

She started to dial a number but he jumped up and pressed his finger on the button to cut her off.

'The only call you are going to make right now is to the emergency dentist. I insist.'

She gave him one of her scariest frowns. It didn't work. He frowned right back at her. And he knew without a shadow of doubt that if they had a frowning competition, he would win.

Yes, Josie might pull her expressive face into some odd shapes sometimes, but it never stayed that way for long. There was always the next emotion bounding along to take its place. Frustration would melt into joy; boredom into excitement.

Whereas he, on the other hand, seemed to have spent the better part of the last decade with a permanent scowl etched on his face. Although, since being based at Elmhurst, he seemed to be losing it. Must be the country air or something.

'All right. All right. I'll go to the dentist.'

She batted his hand away from the phone and started dialling. As she waited for the phone to be answered she looked up at him. 'You have no idea how much I hate it when you get all feudal on me.'

As always, the time for her appointment had scooted past and she was sitting in the waiting room willing her jaw to stop throbbing and flicking through point-less celebrity magazines.

Ever since her very own 'name and shame' feature in one of them all those years ago, she hadn't been able to bear to look at them. Even if, as she sometimes did, she knew the couple on the front who were getting married, announcing their 'baby joy' or pre-senting their new offspring, she was rarely tempted to open up the pages and read more.

But there was only so much staring at dental-hygiene leaflets a girl could do.

She picked up one of the big glossy magazines and started to flick through. It did nothing to ease the in-sistent toothache whatsoever. At least, it didn't until she saw Claire Frazier-Smith staring back at her—or Lady Hammond, as she now was.

Josie smiled. She and Claire had been in the same year at school. She'd been after that man since she was fifteen and almost a decade of persistence had obvi-ously paid off. Lord Hammond had a slightly harried look on his face in the wedding photos. Claire just looked smug in her big white dress.

Josie chuckled then regretted it as another stabbing pain from her tooth brought her back to the present.

She carried on flicking through the photo spread.

The reception looked fantastic, showing off Westbury Castle, the family seat, beautifully. There were shots in the gardens, the ballroom, on the terrace…

And the photos were outstanding. Much better than the portfolio of that turncoat photographer who'd cancelled. She scanned the small print at the bottom of the last photo, checking for the magazine photographer's name.

Josie let the magazine slide off her lap and stared at the blank wall in front of her. It seemed the universe was smiling on her today, opening a window where the Beauforts had slammed a door shut.

It had been a long time, but maybe, just maybe, she might be able to pull in a favour on this one.

The only question was: would Alfie kill her if she suggested it?

The door to his office banged open. Will snapped the point off the pencil he was writing with.

Josie ran into the room, grinning like a loon, and started talking very fast and waving madly with her hands. Well, talking would be a loose definition. She was certainly making noises that sounded like words. The only problem was none of them appeared to be making any sense.

'Josie, Josie! Slow down. I can't understand what you're—'

She launched off again. He picked up the box of tissues from his desk and shoved them in her direction. She stopped mid-sentence. Or at least he thought it was mid-sentence. What the heck had that dentist given her to make her behave like this?

'You're drooling,' he explained.

Josie put her fingers to the corner of her mouth and her eyes widened. She took a tissue and mopped up. While her mouth was otherwise occupied, he took the opportunity to get a few words in himself.

'Just start again from the top. Slowly. OK?'

Josie nodded.

'Ith had ad idea!'

He squinted at her. Oh. 'You've had an idea?'

Her head bobbed up and down violently.

'And a filling, by the looks of it.'

'Old one faw out.'

OK, he was getting the hang of this now. 'The old one fell out.'

She breathed a sigh of relief and sat down in the chair opposite his desk.

'Ith not ease to talk when I numb up to here.' She prodded her left temple with her finger a few times just to make a point.

'And you can't wait twenty minutes until you get the use of your facial muscles back to tell me your idea?'

Vehement shaking of the head. Stupid question, really.

She pulled a tattered magazine out of her bag and prodded the page it was folded over on.

During the next few minutes he managed to gather that she knew the photographer who had taken the pictures and had tried to get in touch both with him and the magazine to see if they would be interested in covering Alfie and Sophie's wedding.

'I sincerely hope you're not planning to call them right now!'

The look was back again. 'Duh!'

Well, it seemed that word was clear in just about all circumstances.

'I email.'

Thank goodness for that.

'Why don't you go and see to it now? We'll chat in an hour or so when you're feeling a bit better.'

'Fanks.' She grinned at him lopsidedly and disappeared back to her own office.

He could see the merit in her idea. Great pictures of the happy couple and absolutely great publicity for Elmhurst Hall, especially its new venture into weddings. It could be just the break they needed. It was a big *if*, though. He'd been going through the figures this afternoon.

All his savings were gone and he'd sold shares, his flat and anything else he could get his hands on to pay for the extensive renovations. Because of the exhibition, they'd added the attics to the project and it had stretched his finances to the limit.

If this wedding was a flop he might as well kiss goodbye to all that cash and pull the plug on the whole thing.

Josie appeared a while later in a much better state to bounce ideas around.

'Have you heard anything back yet?' he asked.

'Not yet, but I'm hopeful.'

'How do you know this photographer person anyway?'

Josie pressed her lips together. 'I knew him back in the days they used to call me *Go-Go Jo*.' She pulled a face and shrugged one shoulder. 'No point in hiding from it. My past is my past and it's a matter of public record.'

'Fair enough.'

'Seems he's reinvented himself and he's doing rather well as *Celebrity Life*'s wedding photographer. I haven't seen him in about six years, but I'd say he owes me a pretty big favour. He made a heck of a lot of money because of me a while back.'

'Why's that?'

She bit her lip and looked down at the desk where she was tracing a finger round a knot in the polished wood.

'He's the one who took that awful photograph of me in the back of the police car.'

CHAPTER TEN

THE bottle of hair dye sat on the bathroom shelf for a good three days. Every time Josie walked past it she picked it up, sighed and put it down again.

With less than a week to go until the wedding, she was just postponing the inevitable. The pink hair had a dark brown stripe an inch wide at the roots.

Tomorrow. She'd do it tomorrow.

After dropping Hattie at school, she made her way back through the gardens. It was beautiful at this time of year. The blazing hot days of August were still to come and the air was warm and golden.

As she made her way down one of the rose-lined paths near the fountain she could see the marquee being erected on the top lawn. And there, standing above the steps that led from the lawn down to the sunken formal garden was Will, staring into space.

She waved at him but he stared straight past and didn't see her.

Only when she reached the bottom of the stone staircase did he look in her direction. She waved again.

'I was looking out for you,' he said.

'You weren't doing a very good job of it. I've been waving my arm off trying to attract your attention.'

His gaze drifted off into the distance again. 'Sorry.'

'What are you doing out here? Inspecting the marquee?'

He jerked his head round to look at it. 'Oh. No. It looks very nice, though.'

'Will?'

'There's no other way to say this. I've got to go away and I'm not sure if I'll be back in time for the wedding.'

Not here for the wedding? But they'd sweated blood and tears to get this far! She needed him here. More than that, she wanted him here, so they could share in the triumph together when they pulled it off.

'My grandmother called. Her house has been burgled and she's in a terrible state.'

Josie's hand flew to cover her mouth. 'That's awful! Of course you should go to her.'

'I know.'

He looked so forlorn. What was the matter? She didn't like seeing him like this. He was more than just a colleague now; he was her friend. They'd managed to keep the chemistry between them to a damp fizz. Mostly. Well, OK, it was still there, but they'd learnt to work together in spite of it, both realising it was utter foolishness to go down that road.

'Don't you get on?'

He smiled a grim smile. 'No, we get on famously—

as long as I don't give her any cheek, as she calls it. It's just…I should be here. The coffers are well and truly empty after all the extra work we've done to bring the facilities up to standard for a wedding venue. It's my duty to stay and see it through.'

'Rubbish.'

Lines creased his forehead. 'I beg your pardon.'

She took his arm and practically dragged him back towards the hall, which was no mean feat considering the difference in their sizes. 'I'm afraid that you've read those publicity brochures too many times and have started believing your own hype, Lord Radcliffe.'

'Don't be ridiculous.'

'Duty shouldn't be to bricks and mortar, even if they are arranged in such a wonderful fashion as they are in this place. Your loyalty should be to flesh and blood—the people who care about you. The people you love.'

'Don't you need me here? What if something goes wrong?'

Josie waved a dismissive hand. 'I'll be fine. We've planned this wedding to within an inch of its life, haven't we? I'm sure I can handle a few last-minute hiccups.'

He grabbed her by both shoulders. 'Thank you, Josie. You're a star.' Then he kissed her firmly and quickly on the lips and ran off into the hall.

She stood there, right where he'd left her, for at least three minutes before she moved. By the time she reached the offices he'd gone.

The offices seemed awfully quiet as she sat at her

desk that afternoon. More than once she started to jump up and head across the corridor to tell him something, only to flump back down into her chair when she remembered he wouldn't be there.

Later, after she'd picked up Hattie from school and returned to the cottage, she made her way to the bathroom and picked up the box of hair dye. There was no point putting it off any longer.

The little parish church in the grounds of Elmhurst Hall hadn't seen this much activity since the village baby boom of 1997 when the vicar had baptised ten babies in one day.

With only two hours to go until the ceremony, Josie was getting tired of trying to run in three directions at once. She walked down the central aisle of the church and checked the end of each pew. The posies fastened there were all identical and perfect.

The mobile phone in her pocket beeped and vibrated.

She was waiting for a call from the photographer, the company that was doing the wedding video and one of the bridesmaids who had got lost and was periodically ringing in for the next set of directions.

It wasn't any of them. She knew this ring tone. She waited and let it go to voicemail. The only thing she would get if she answered this call was earache—her mother wanting to know why she wasn't back up at the hall being primped and plucked and hairsprayed to within an inch of her life.

Another walk round. Just thirty more minutes checking everything was set. Then she'd go and sacrifice herself to the tortuous ritual of getting ready to be a bridesmaid.

She jogged out of the church and through a gap in the hedge. The little church of St Stephen's was situated on the edge of the Elmhurst estate, close to the village. If you knew the right place to look, you could cut out a five-minute walk down through the lych-gate and back up the drive through the main gate to the hall and pop out beside the rose garden.

She picked up speed and ran along the high terrace overlooking the fountains and flowerbeds and made her way to the top lawn.

The marquee looked spectacular. The inside was draped with acres of pleated ivory fabric and vast floral displays hung over each of the circular tables, trailing ivy down to almost touch the tablecloth. And there seemed to be fairy lights and candles everywhere. This evening, after the formal dinner, there was going to be dancing and it would look just magical as Alfie and Sophie took to the floor.

She smiled and backed out of the marquee, savouring the picture of peace and calm, knowing that mayhem would follow shortly. It was worth a little stress to get this wedding perfect for Alfie. He'd always been there as a referee between her and her parents and it was about time she repaid him somehow.

Her mobile rang again and this time she answered it.

The photographer. 'Jeff? Where are you?'

'I'm parked in the little lane just down beside the church. Shall I meet you by the church entrance?'

'OK. See you there in five.'

Back across the terrace she ran, ignoring another call from her mother as she jogged. Once more through the hedge and round the path to the front of the church.

'Jeff!'

'Where do you want me?' he said with a wicked grin that meant she could take that any way she liked.

'Anywhere you think will produce a good shot,' she answered. 'Come inside and have a quick scout round. There's a place near the choir stalls that's not too obtrusive and should give you a good view. I really appreciate you agreeing to do this at the last minute.'

He shrugged. 'The magazine pays well, and any time I managed to take a photo of you at a party, it always turned out rather well for me.'

She gave him a firm look. 'I promise you this is Alfie's big day and I'm not going to be doing anything in the least shocking. I've given it up for Lent.'

'Lent was months ago.'

She winked at him. 'Just goes to prove what an exceptionally good girl I'm being these days.'

He chuckled.

'Seriously, Jeff. You are going to behave yourself, aren't you? Official photographs only.'

'I'll tell you what, Lady Josephine. I'll behave if you do.'

* * *

'At last! Do you know how many times I've tried to phone you in the last hour?'

Josie bit her lip to stop herself from saying 'five'.

'Sorry, Mum. It's a bit harem-scarem this morning. My feet have hardly touched the ground.'

'Well, they'd better come back down to earth and stop here right now. All the others are ready bar the headdresses.'

'Did Belinda get here in time?'

Her mother scowled and summoned a shaggy-looking man Josie assumed was the hairdresser with a click of her fingers. 'Well before you, Josephine. And that's saying something, considering she almost ended up in Canterbury. She and Clarissa have taken the little bridesmaids for a walk down the corridor to look out of the window to try and get rid of some of their restless energy.'

Josie looked around the wood-panelled living room of what had once been Harry's and now was Will's apartment. He'd very kindly offered the bridal party the use of his rooms as all the guest rooms in the private part of the hall were a bit damp and dusty. They'd be dealt with in phase two of the renovations, if that day ever came.

Josie outmanoeuvred her mother, managed to avoid being sat down and fussed over by the hairdresser and knocked on the door of the bedroom.

The voice from behind the door was small and shaky. 'Come in.'

She pushed it open and peered round.

'Sophie? Are you OK?'

Sophie was sitting on the edge of a large oak four-poster. She nodded hard while looking at the carpet. Her blonde hair was swept back meticulously and she held a small tiara in her hands.

'Why don't you let me put that on for you?'

Sophie looked up at her with a face full of horror. 'Oh, no! Nobody's allowed to touch my hair except Gavin or your mother.'

Josie held her hands up in a gesture of surrender. 'OK, OK! I promise I will keep at least two feet away from the tiara at all times.'

Sophie didn't smile, but at least she didn't look ready to bolt any more.

'Don't worry, Sophie. Everything is coming along smoothly. It'll all be fine.'

'Thank you.' The shaky voice had been downgraded to a squeak.

Josie sat down on the bed, close enough to offer comfort, but far enough away not to rumple the bride too badly. 'Alfie is going to faint when he sees you. You look gorgeous.'

'Really?'

'Of course. Mind you, I think Alfie would think you looked smashing in a garden sack. He's madly in love with you.'

The tiniest of smiles chased a few worry lines off Sophie's forehead. 'He is, isn't he?'

Josie nodded. 'Now, you just focus on that and let

the rest of us worry about the details. It's going to be a wonderful day.'

'Sophie!' The screech from the neighbouring room almost sent the poor bride scurrying into the *en suite* bathroom. The girl was quivering with fright. 'Time to fix that tiara on!'

Sophie rubbed her head. 'I still have holes in my scalp from the last attempt.'

'Just ask Gavin—is that his name?—to do it. He doesn't look like he's got the strength to do any real damage.'

Sophie looked hopeful. 'Do you think she'd let him?'

Josie sighed. The thought of marrying back into all of this sent shivers down her spine. Not in a million years.

'I'll tell you what, I'll create a distraction. You nip in there while she's tackling me.'

Sophie nodded. Her face was so serious that Josie wanted to laugh.

'Ready?'

The bride stood and walked towards the bedroom door.

Josie readied her lungs and gave her mother a yell. 'Mother? I think I may have forgotten to bring any underwear.'

The door flew open and the sight of her mother even made Josie shiver a little. She took a few steps into the room and fixed Josie with a withering stare. Sophie, standing by the door, was frozen to the spot.

'Go,' Josie mouthed to her and waved her along with a hand.

Sophie didn't need to be told twice.

Josie turned her attention back to her mother. 'Can we improvise, Mum?' she said, pulling open the nearest drawer to discover a neat row of silk boxer shorts all folded in half. She shut the drawer quickly again. Borrowing her boss's underpants was something even she wouldn't do.

She felt the heat of a blush climbing up her neck and hoped to heaven her mother didn't notice. She might guess this was all a ruse and Sophie needed a few more minutes with Gavin.

'What on earth do you mean, you haven't got any knickers? What are you wearing now?'

Josie wiggled her eyebrows.

'Really, Josephine! You are the limit! I told you to pack spare everythings in the bag you brought up from the cottage.'

Josie walked towards the portable coat rack that held her bridesmaid's dress. 'Tell you what, Mum. Why don't you check on the little ones while I have a look and get changed?'

Her mother glowered at her then swept from the room.

She heard a muffled, 'Why, Sophie. That tiara looks lovely.'

Mission accomplished.

'Oh, look!' she yelled through the open door. 'I did bring some emergency knickers after all.'

Josie started shedding clothes and decided to hop in the shower for two minutes just to get clean and fresh-smelling. As long as she was careful not to get her hair wet it would be OK.

Ten minutes later there was a knock on the door.

'Mum? Is that you? I need someone to lace me up.'

The bridesmaid's outfits were in two pieces. There was a long A-line skirt, kind of Edwardian in shape, and a bodice that laced up over the top. They'd gone for the raspberry crush instead of the mint-green and, much to Josie's surprise, it really suited her colouring.

She was just admiring her cleavage when she heard a hushed voice.

'Mummy?'

She spun round to see Hattie standing in the doorway wearing a full-skirted dress in a matching colour and looking the most angelic thing that had ever walked the face of this earth.

'Sweetheart, you look scrumptious!'

Hattie grinned. 'I can spin in this dress. Look!' She twirled round and round with her arms out wide, her smile glowing brighter and brighter. One of Hattie's only requirements for her wardrobe was that her dresses would 'spin'.

'You'd better stop that before you feel sick, sweetie.'

Hattie slowed down and patted the dress back into place. Then she took a good long look at Josie.

'Mummy,' she said, with a wobble in her voice, 'you look like a princess.'

Josie was tempted to bawl. From Hattie, that was

the highest praise possible. So what if she was going to blend into the crowd and be normal? She wanted to see that look in her daughter's eyes again and again.

Her mother appeared at the doorway and gave a little *humph*. 'About time too. Let's get those laces done up.'

'Just remember I've got to breathe as well, OK?'

Her mother walked behind her and gave an almighty tug on the strings. 'Nonsense, Josephine. Breathing is for wimps, haven't you heard?'

Josie blinked twice and twisted round to look at her mother.

'What?' her mother said with a naughty smile. 'You think you're the only one allowed to crack jokes around here?'

A surprised giggle erupted from her mouth and she covered her lips with her hand as another followed.

Her mother was nothing if not quick. Within two minutes she was fully-laced and still breathing. Just.

'All done?'

Her mother raised her eyebrows. 'Not quite. What on earth are we going to do with that hair of yours?'

Will ran through the rose garden, down the drive to the main gate and up the path that led to the doorway of St Stephen's Church. He knew about Josie's hole in the hedge, but there was no way he was taking a short cut.

He was praying the bride was going to be traditionally late and, as he slipped into a space on one of the back rows, he was relieved to find she was sticking to tradition.

He'd only just sat down and caught his breath when he heard shuffling and voices outside. The bridal party must be assembling. His heart began to beat faster.

It was only nerves about the wedding, that was all. Nothing else.

They'd been planning this for three months and a lot was riding on it. Anyone would be a little jumpy under those circumstances.

The organ started playing something classical he recognised but couldn't remember the name of and his heart doubled speed. He stood, and tried to tell himself he should just stare straight ahead. That he wasn't looking out for anyone in particular.

With great effort, he marshalled his features and focused on the groom waiting in the front pew. Before he knew it, a gaggle of females in dark pink dresses swept past. But where was Josie? Was everything OK? Was she having to deal with some last-minute disaster on her own?

Sophie and her father were now making painfully slow progress down the aisle. Step, together. Step, together. He could practically see the bride mouthing the words. She must be so terrified of racing down to the front that she was going half-speed.

And blocking his way.

He could hardly elbow past her and sprint out of the church, could he?

Finally, just as she was about to join the groom at the front of the church, and while the organ music would drown the sound of his shoes on the stone floor, he shoved his order of service behind a bible on the little shelf in front of him and crept out of the church.

He sprinted away from the lych-gate and dived through the hole in the hedge that Josie had pointed out to him. At least, he'd thought it was the hole. All he got was a faceful of branch.

He stood back, took a good look at the hedge and tried again, only to burst through so hard he almost stumbled and fell over onto the grassy terrace overlooking the formal garden.

He found his equilibrium and stared this way and that, trying to guess where she might be. Before he'd made up his mind, his feet were racing in the direction of the huge marquee.

He skidded inside and searched the faces of the waiters and waitresses. Barrett was in one corner, giving a last-minute lesson on proper silver-service etiquette to a group of young men dressed in black and white. Will jogged over and didn't wait for a gap in the conversation.

'Where's Josie? Have you seen her?' he managed between pants.

Barrett's excellent training came to the forefront as he didn't bat an eyelash at the interruption.

'Is she not with the bridal party, sir?'

Will shook his head and dashed out of the marquee. He tried the kitchens, the tearoom, even the cottage. Josie was not here. It was as if she'd disappeared off the face of the earth. And that meant that this wedding was a runaway boat with no one at the helm.

He dashed back to the church and as he rounded the corner he saw the great wooden doors opening and the strains of the 'Bridal March' bellowing from the organ. He rested his hands on his bent thighs and dragged in some much-needed oxygen. He didn't know exactly why he'd come back here, only that it seemed the most sensible place to be.

Alfie and Sophie posed at the church door for the photographer, blinking as their eyes adjusted to the bright July afternoon. Why was there always someone in the way when he needed to get in and out of the church?

After what seemed like an age, they moved forward and the rest of the wedding party spilled out after them.

He was just about to turn and race off again in the direction of the hall, but something caught his eye, a familiar cheeky smile and a bright pair of laughing eyes.

The little air he'd managed to pull back into his lungs evacuated.

Josie?

She was…she was…well, stunning. That was what she was.

Gone was the luminous pink shock of hair, but he still couldn't take his eyes off her. In its place was beautiful dark chestnut hair, swept into a glossy hairstyle studded with flowers at the back.

And the dress. Oh, my goodness.

If he'd thought the 'Pink Lady' waitress outfit was bad for his blood pressure, this one was probably going to finish him off. The bodice of the dress was tight and revealed an hourglass figure that was positively illegal. The funky, pink-haired Josie was fun to be around and intriguing, but this new, classy Josie was dangerous.

Dangerous, because he was thinking he would never be able to look at her the same way again. Dangerous, because he'd been holding on to his composure by a thread when she was around and he thought the thread had just snapped.

She still stood out from the crowd, in an elegant, quirky, Audrey Hepburn kind of way. He looked around. The other guests were slowly flowing out of the church, swirling around her, laughing and talking to each other. Were they blind? Why hadn't they stopped in their tracks the way he had?

She turned and saw him. Ignoring the photographer's plea that she hold it for just one more shot, she picked up her skirts and lightly ran to his side.

'Will? What are you doing here?'

He gasped. He gaped. He said nothing.

Her face took on a look of real concern. 'Has something happened…to your grandmother?'

He shook his head.

'Then why are you back here?'

Because you needed me. Because I couldn't stay away.

He held up a hand. 'Give me a second,' he croaked. 'I've been running.'

Well, it was true. It just wasn't the reason he was

having trouble exchanging oxygen for carbon dioxide at the moment.

'Did you bump into a wheelbarrow?'

'Huh?'

'Never mind. Just a wild guess.'

She reached up and threaded the fingers of her left hand, the one that wasn't holding a bouquet, through the front of his hair. That didn't help the situation in the slightest. He'd completely forgotten what he was going to say now.

She removed a bit of yew branch, showed it to him then threw it away.

'Josephine! Will you come here this instant?'

Josie looked towards the crowd outside the church. Her mother was standing slightly apart from the others, hands on hips.

Josie shrugged. 'Gotta go and say "cheese" again. I'll see you later. As soon as I can get away.'

CHAPTER ELEVEN

As it turned out, 'later' was a lot, lot later. After the service, there were the photographs, a minor crisis with the wine delivery, flower girls that needed to be rounded up and shepherded and lots of smiling and greeting. Yawn.

Now and again she saw Will hovering near the section of the marquee that led to the food-preparation area, talking to Barrett, who was doing a sterling job as master of ceremonies, but every time she had a spare moment something popped up or he disappeared.

And here she was, stranded on the top table, feeling as if she were on display as she pretended to eat her food. Not that it didn't look gorgeous. It was just that she'd been living and breathing this menu for weeks, from each change of dessert to the choice of wine, and she was thoroughly sick of the thought of it. And even if she was tempted to take a bite, her curiosity damped down her appetite.

What was Will doing back here? Was everything OK? He'd looked mighty odd earlier on in the churchyard.

A flash of pink streaked past the table. And then another one.

Sophie's nieces, the other flower girls, were twins and a complete handful. And, since the chief bridesmaid was more interested in flirting with the best man, keeping them under control had fallen to Josie. Heaven knew where their mother was. Probably hiding behind her rather large hat and pretending she wasn't related to them.

Josie quickly squeezed her way behind the row of chairs at the top table and scanned the room for anything four feet high and dressed in raspberry crush. They were eighteen months older than Hattie—not that you'd think it from the way they acted.

She caught sight of two giggling faces on the other side of the marquee and gave chase just in time to see them disappear under a table. Suddenly, people were jumping up out of their seats and dropping cutlery.

She made it to table twelve before the twins had a chance to untangle themselves from the legs underneath and was ready and waiting for them when they emerged, snickering.

'Right! You two come with me.'

She was tempted to lead them away by the ear, but settled for a firm grip on each hand. Only, with a daughter as quiet and sedate as Hattie, she underestimated the wriggliness of seven-year-olds who were used to getting their own way.

A few seconds later they had escaped and were heading in the direction of an exit on the far side of

the room. The rest of the guests seemed to be oblivi-
ous, too busy swilling champagne and stuffing their
faces, but she was aware of her mother's eyes on her
and resisted the urge to pick up her skirts and sprint
after them. Hopefully, Mum wouldn't object to a
ladylike trot.

They exited the main room of the marquee and
skipped into a side-room where waiters were
readying crates of champagne for the toasts. The
wedding cake stood alone in one corner, waiting for
its moment of glory.

Jade and Amber, the terrible twins, were closing in
on the cake. But, instead of looking where they were
going, they were looking over their shoulders and
giggling at her as she chased them.

Josie slowed to a brisk walk. Maybe if she stopped
pursuing them, they'd slow down too.

Her heart was beating fast and her breath was
coming in short puffs. Not just from the chase, but
also from the thought of that cake coming crashing to
the ground. Those two little tikes were not going to
ruin this wedding! She couldn't bear the look on her
mother's face if it all went pear-shaped.

The plan was working. Jade and Amber slowed
down and started whispering to each other. Josie kept
a careful pace and was just about to shoot an arm out
to lay hold of one of them when they took off again—
straight into the table that held the cake.

It teetered. Josie held her breath.

Amber and Jade froze then promptly burst into

tears. Not that Josie thought they were in the least bit sorry. They just seemed to be afraid of getting told off.

The cake rocked slightly and looked as if it was going to find its centre of balance when she noticed that one of the pillars supporting the top layer of the four-tiered cake was wonky and threatening to tip over at any moment.

She lunged towards the cake, hands thrust outwards, but she was too far away. It was going to…

From nowhere a deft pair of hands shot out and caught the top tier as it plummeted towards the floor.

It was Will! Never had she been so grateful for his ability to move with such efficiency.

The elaborate decoration of sugar flowers on top wasn't quite as lucky as the cake. Even as Will's hands brought the cake to a stop, they carried on sliding. A split-second later there was a shattering sound and a hundred petal fragments littered the floor.

Before Josie could even think about how to fix any of the less damaged flowers back together, Jade's little hand reached out, picked up the one undamaged sugar lily and popped it into her mouth. Amber scooped up a few of the larger broken pieces and copied her sister. Then they took one look at Josie's face and scarpered.

She turned to Will, who was still holding the cake away from himself as if it were an unexploded bomb.

'What…what do I do with this?' he stammered.

'Don't make any sudden moves.'

His gaze, which had been fixed intently on the cake, flickered to her.

'Sorry. Bad habit. When I'm in deep trouble, I quip.'

He gave her a look that said, *No, really?*

'Give it to me.'

He carefully handed over the small tier, making sure he didn't catch any of the delicate royal-icing swirls on the edges of his cuffs. Josie placed it on the trolley next to the headless cake.

'That was very good timing, Lord Radcliffe. How did you appear out of nowhere so suddenly?'

'I was watching the chase. When they neared the cake, I thought I'd better move. Fast.'

'I'm very glad you did.'

'Even if the cake has survived, the decorations are unsalvageable. What are we going to do? We can't serve this up. If pictures of this go out in that celebrity magazine, we might as well kiss goodbye to the whole "Weddings at Elmhurst" idea. It's the worst kind of advertising we could have hoped for.'

Josie stared hard at the cake.

'I was thinking we could leave the top tier off, but it looks out of proportion without it. The decorations on the lower levels aren't big enough to make a convincing top-of-the-cake display. And it's not as if there are any spare flowers hanging around…'

She spun round to face him.

'Will, I need you to run to the offices, get a stack of copier paper and some pencils and pens.'

'But—'

'No time to argue. Just go!' she said, giving him a hefty shove in the right direction.

* * *

Josie walked primly back to the top table, smiling at other guests as she went, but avoided getting sucked into conversations, picked up her bouquet and quickly left the main marquee.

Once back with the cake, she quickly unravelled the ribbon holding the stems of the flowers together and pulled the arrangement apart. Much to her disappointment at the time, Sophie had veered away from her suggestion of minimalist bouquets of trumpet lilies tied together with a wide band of ribbon and had opted for fussy, trailing arrangements. Thank goodness the bride hadn't listened to her.

Even her bridesmaid's bouquet was full of different flowers and bits of greenery, all individually wired.

She stuck her head round the entrance to the main section of the marquee. The speeches hadn't started yet. She had a bit of time. And if Sophie's father was true to form, he'd bellow on for a good twenty minutes, giving her even more precious seconds.

She started grouping pieces of the bouquet together to make an arrangement of real flowers for the top of the cake. Why have the pasty-looking sugar variety when you could have the real thing?

Ten minutes later she stepped back to survey her handiwork.

She pulled a face. It definitely was Picasso-inspired—stylish in its own way, but lopsided and avant-garde.

There was no way she was going to pull this off. It was beyond her capabilities. If only she'd gone to finishing-school as her mother had wanted her to. She'd have been able to whip up a stunning concoction of flowers in no time.

There was only one solution. One that meant swallowing a lump of pride as big as the cake sitting next to her. In one go.

She looked at the cake then back at her expressionist flower arrangement. There really was no choice.

As predicted, Sophie's father was boring the pants off everybody. She slipped into the main marquee and crept up to the top table.

'Mum,' she whispered through her teeth, smiling at the same time.

Her mother turned round. *What now?* was written all over her face.

'I need your help.'

The look of annoyance was replaced with one of shock. 'What did you just say?'

'I need you.'

Her mother's eyes widened. 'You? Need *me*?'

Josie nodded, still grinning, hoping anyone watching would think they were murmuring praise at the speech. Her mother slid gracefully out of her chair and glided out of the room behind Josie, whose exit was not nearly so ladylike. She led her mother to the cake and did a *ta-dah* gesture with her hands.

'How on earth did that happen?'

'Sabotage,' she said grimly. 'The sugar flowers from on top of the cake are history.' She decided not to add that they were probably being digested at this very moment by Jade and Amber, who were now sitting next to their mother and looking sweetly angelic.

'I tried to improvise with my bouquet, but it all turned out a bit wrong.'

Her mother was already picking apart her arrangement, shaking her head.

'It wasn't my fault, Mum. Not this time.'

Her mother didn't take her eyes off the flowers she was carefully gathering together. 'I know, Josephine. Actually, this was very quick thinking.'

Now it was Josie's turn to raise her eyebrows.

'Thanks,' she said slowly, eyeing her mother suspiciously and waiting for the sting in the tail.

But dear old Mum was too busy picking out bits of leaves and grass and delicate flowers to go with a central lily to respond. And when she'd finished that, she made smaller swathes from the remnants to replace the sugar flowers on the other tiers.

By the time the best man's speech had started the cake was looking fabulous again. Even better, in fact, because the colour of the real flowers looked stunning against the stiff ivory icing.

Josie smiled at her mother. Her mother's eyes crinkled in return.

'Thanks, Mum. I owe you.'

'Nonsense.' Her mother swept a stray tendril of Josie's hair behind one ear. 'You've done a splendid job of this wedding and I wouldn't want to see all your hard work wasted and Alfie and Sophie's day ruined.'

Without warning, tears filled Josie's eyes.

'Now, stop that nonsense at once,' her mother said, reaching for the handkerchief in her pocket and dabbing under her eyes. 'The best man will be toasting the bridesmaids in a minute and it would be rude to turn up looking like a panda.'

Josie was just about to follow her mother back to her place at the top table when Will stumbled in, clutching assorted stationery to his chest.

'I must say I'm intrigued. How on earth are you going to fix a cake with pencils and paper...? Oh.'

He looked at the cake and then at the pads and pencils he was holding.

'What are all these for, then?'

'Your job,' she said, leading him to an empty table, 'is to find anything in there under the age of ten and bring them out here to do colouring and drawing. Tell them it's a competition.'

'Me? Look after children?'

Josie put her hands on her hips. 'Well, I can't do it. I've got to go and be toasted.'

Will just stared at her and dropped the pads and pencils onto the table with a clatter. She skipped off towards the main reception room but turned back just before she crossed the threshold.

'And, Will?'

He was still frozen to the spot.

She winked at him. 'You do know you're providing the prize, don't you? Make it a good one.'

* * *

Guests were mingling, drinking champagne on the lawn, as the marquee was being prepared for an evening of dancing and celebration. Will, finally free of his babysitting duty, was holding Hattie's small hand and searching the crowd for Josie.

It wasn't long before he spotted her. And he realised he'd fallen into the habit of always locating her when he walked into a room.

Hattie broke free and ran to her.

Will longed to do the same, but it was neither the time nor the place. This was business. He had to remember that. And she was Josie, the kooky it-girl-turned-waitress who despised all this formality and fakery. Although it was hard to remember that when she so obviously fitted in.

He watched her chatting effortlessly with some of the titled guests, her champagne glass swaying to and fro as she told a story.

It was also getting hard to remember why it was a bad idea to get involved with her. OK, technically, she was his employee, but he never seemed to think of her that way. She was his friend, his equal, his partner.

'Super wedding, William.'

He watched Josie a few seconds longer then turned round.

'Lady Beaufort. A pleasure to have you here. I hope you are enjoying it.'

She smiled and there was a grudging light in her eyes. 'You've been very lucky it all fell into place,' she said and took a sip of her champagne, keeping her eyes on him all the time. 'That girl is a liability.'

Will's spine stiffened. 'Luck has nothing to do with it. She worked very hard.'

Beatrice laughed gently and patted his arm. 'There's no escaping genetics, is there? First your grandfather and now you. You know what they say about apples not falling far from the tree…'

He felt the fire rise from his stomach and boil in his chest. Josie was no showgirl, working in a seedy club. And even if she were, it wouldn't matter. She was a lady, in every definition of the word. More than this woman standing in front of him would ever be.

'Of course, you wouldn't be stupid enough to take up with her, would you? With her reputation… The family couldn't be brought into disrepute again. It just wouldn't do.'

Will's eyes narrowed.

'You do get my point, William dear, don't you?'

'Perfectly.'

Will sat on one of the stone walls of the fountain in the centre of the formal garden, criss-crossed by paths through the flower beds. He watched the sun disappear behind the trees to the west. The noise of the party was removed, floating on the wind.

Wedding guests laughed and talked and danced to the big-band music Sophie and Alfie had insisted on. It all seemed somewhere in a different universe, a figment of his imagination that might fade away if he turned round too quickly.

It wasn't fair what they were doing to Josie. Everyone deserved a second chance. And she'd more than proved herself. But he was learning, in these circles, with these people, that one chance was all anyone got.

A slow creeping realisation swept over him. This was what she hated. This feeling of being a tiny pawn in somebody else's game. No wonder she'd run away, pushed so hard against anything that reminded her of it.

He'd foolishly thought that accepting the title of Lord Radcliffe, becoming part of these élite social circles, would give him the freedom, the acceptance he'd been so eagerly searching for all his life.

Instead it had done the opposite and if he didn't know that Piers Beaufort would neglect this wonderful building and destroy his legacy, ruining countless lives, he'd hand it all to them on a silver platter tomorrow.

He stood up, brushed the grit off the backs of his trousers and headed towards the source of all the music and light that had been taunting him for the past half-hour. As he walked up the stone steps to the top lawn, he spotted a little pink figure sobbing, her arms folded on top of her knees and her face buried in the front of her dress.

'Hattie?'

The little girl sniffed and looked up.

Will moved to sit beside her. 'What's up?'

Hattie shook her head and buried it in her lap again.

He sat there in silence. 'Do you want me to get Mummy?'

She shook her head, just once.

'Do you want me to get Grandma?'

The sobbing started up again, accompanied by vigorous head-shaking.

He was on his own. But he had no idea of how to solve a little girl's problems. He only knew how to solve business-type problems. In those sorts of cases, he'd go through a process of elimination, trying to pinpoint the source of the trouble. He shrugged, although no one was around to see it. What the heck?

'Hattie, have you hurt yourself?'

'No.' The word was muffled through layers of pink fabric.

'Has someone been horrible to you?'

Nothing. OK, he might be on to something here.

'Did someone say something to upset you?'

The crying got harder. He scooped her off the step and into his lap.

'Who was it?'

She took a huge, gulping breath. 'J-J-Jade and Amber.'

'What did they say?'

'They said I...I couldn't be a proper princess because I didn't know how to dance.'

Will smiled. 'That's rubbish. I've seen you dancing around in the gardens and it looked lovely.'

She looked up at him and gave him a withering, five-year-old, that's-what-you-know look. 'No. Not that kind of dancing. Proper dancing. Amber said real princesses know how to schmaltz.'

Will raised his eyebrows.

'Do you mean *waltz*?'

Hattie thought for a second then nodded.

'And I suppose Amber and Jade know how to waltz?'

'Yes. Their mummy sent them to lessons. I only do ballet.'

'Ballet is proper dancing too; it's just a different kind of dancing.'

Hattie shrugged. Those twins had a lot to answer for.

'Well, I think you just might be a princess anyway. Let me get out my princess check-list.'

He sat Hattie back on the step and pretended to get a long piece of rolled-up paper and a pen from his inside pocket. The little girl stared at him with round eyes.

Will swallowed. He hoped he was doing the right thing. No choice but to go for it now.

'Let's see…' He made a show of inspecting Hattie's long dark hair. 'Long, flowing tresses…check!' And he made an imaginary tick in an imaginary box on the imaginary piece of paper.

Hattie put a nervous hand to her hair.

'Eyes that sparkle and shine…' Will got nose to nose with Hattie and took a good look into her eyes, keeping his face very serious '…check!'

She began to giggle.

'Beautiful ballgown…check! Feet delicate enough to fit into a glass slipper…'

Somehow thinking of Hattie's feet led him to

thinking of Josie's feet, which led him inevitably to thinking of Josie's ankles. He sighed.

He felt a tugging on his sleeve. 'Are my feet too big, Will?'

'No. No, they're perfect. Check! You look like a princess to me.'

Hattie smiled.

'And I should know. I'm Lord Radcliffe and Amber and Jade are both just "Honourable Miss". Come on.'

He stood up and held out his hand. Hattie looked worried.

'Where are we going?'

'To show the Honourable Misses how it's done.'

With that, he picked Hattie up, smiling at her squeal of joy, and waltzed across the lawn with her.

Once they stopped spinning in order to enter the marquee, Hattie stared at him in wonder. 'You know how to do proper dancing,' she said, with a kind of awe in her voice.

'Well, my grandma was a dancer. When I was little she taught me how to waltz.' Thankfully, she hadn't included some of the other dances she knew in his lessons.

'So now you have a prince to dance with. You must be a princess. Do Amber and Jade have princes to dance with?' he asked as they reached the dance floor and he began spinning round with her again. Nan would have been proud of his footwork.

Hattie peeked over his shoulder to where the twins were watching, hands on hips and noses clearly out of joint. 'No. They've only got their older brothers to dance with. And Christopher smells of cabbage.'

Will laughed and dipped Hattie backwards into a waltz pose so she squealed and giggled.

Josie's heart squeezed and a lump rose in her throat. How had she ever thought that man stuffy and unfeeling?

Just the look on Hattie's face almost brought a tear to her eye.

She'd overheard the argument between Hattie and the twins and had been racing everywhere trying to find her daughter after she'd run off, tears streaming down her face. She'd been on the verge of properly panicking when she'd spotted Will and Hattie twirling on the dance floor. And now her heart was beating hard for an entirely different reason.

The music finished and she approached the pair as they slowed to a stop.

Will turned and smiled at her. 'It looks as if Mummy wants a go. Why don't you go with Grandma and have some of that delicious cake? There are strawberries too—as big as golf balls. I saw them.'

Hattie wriggled down from Will's hold and ran off in the direction of the buffet table. Josie was going to say something, although she wasn't sure exactly what, but before the words could form an orderly queue in her mind Will had slipped one hand round her waist, taken hold of the other and was leading her round the dance floor.

After a minute or two she said, 'You're quite good at this, aren't you?'

He smiled. 'You're not so bad yourself.'

'I'm not doing anything. All I'm doing is following your lead and co-operating.'

She saw his pupils flare. 'Oh, you're doing much more than that.'

For the first time in her life she was stuck for a smart answer, so she clamped her lips together and just let the music flow round her, let Will's hands and feet guide her anywhere he wanted to go. It didn't matter where. She was safe with him.

'What happened about your grandmother?' she finally asked.

'The police aren't sure she was actually burgled. Nothing seems to have been taken. It's quite possible she just went out and forgot to shut the door behind her.'

'Does she do that sort of thing a lot?'

Will shook his head. 'It was the anniversary of my grandfather's death two days ago. Even though it was such a long time ago, it still gets to her. She often gets quite emotional at this time of year.'

Josie stiffened in his arms. 'What? And you left her to come back here and play the gracious host? You really didn't listen to anything I said the other day, did you?'

Will gave her an indulgent look. 'What kind of man do you think I am? Of course I didn't leave her alone. She's come back here with me for a visit. I thought she could do with a break.'

Of course he did. Why had she expected anything else of him? Of course Will would do the right thing. It was the way he was made. Just as, in the same way, she seemed to be wired to do the opposite.

Which reminded her. This dress was starting to stop her lungs inflating properly and the shoes were giving her blisters. At least, she hoped it was the dress that was constricting her lungs. The other option was entirely too complicated.

She stopped looking into Will's eyes and looked around the room. There was nothing left to be done. The cake had been cut and served. The buffet was on the table. The bar was still flowing.

The music softened and the waltz drew to a close. Over the dying strains she heard the announcement that it was time to wave off the bride and groom. Slowly the greater proportion of the guests made their way out into the courtyard, where a car, which had once been a rather nice Jaguar, was covered in so much paper, balloons and tin cans it looked like a giant decorated toilet roll.

Sophie and Alfie appeared, looking more relaxed than they had in weeks. It wasn't until they were standing in a semicircle round the car and waiting for the grinning Sophie to toss her bouquet that she realised Will's hand was still round her waist.

She didn't know how to feel about that.

She should be horrified. He should be looking for Miss Sensible to help him produce a brood of heirs, not flirting with her. Not that Will was exactly flirting.

She didn't know quite how to label it. Something was bubbling under the surface between them.

Before she had time to work out what that something might be, she saw Sophie turn her back and get ready to hurl the bouquet. Josie backed away, guessing the trajectory would bring it far too close for comfort, but there were lines of other wedding guests behind her and Will now and there wasn't really anywhere to go.

Flowers were sailing through the air, pieces of greenery dropping out. Josie tried to duck and turn away, but it was no good. The bouquet hit her on the side of the head with a thwack then dropped into Will's waiting hands.

She rubbed her face and turned to look at him. He was still frozen to the spot, for all the world looking like one of the statues in the garden, shock on his face and a ragged arrangement of lilies in his hands.

The other guests cheered and clapped and, for the first time since she was about thirteen, Josie blushed.

'Rather you than me,' she said.

CHAPTER TWELVE

THANKFULLY, the attention of the gathered guests turned to the departing bride and groom and, as people edged forward to wave and shout their congratulations, Josie and Will found themselves alone at the back of the crowd.

She laughed. He was still holding the bouquet, shell-shocked. That just made her laugh even harder.

'You know what, Will?'

'What?' He put the flowers behind his back and straightened himself.

'We did it!' A grin took hold of her mouth so wide she thought her face would split.

Will lost his stunned look and grinned back. 'We did, didn't we?'

'The wedding was a success.'

'You were a success,' he said, sobering slightly.

Josie couldn't resist bouncing slightly on the balls of her feet, even if it did aggravate the blisters. 'And it would be so much easier to handle if family weren't involved. I think we can really do this, Will.'

And then, since it seemed to be the thing her brain

did best when she was attracted to someone, she did something really stupid. She took advantage of Will's hands being behind his back, grabbed his face, pulled him towards her and kissed him.

She had only meant it to be a brief kiss, a celebratory peck, but somehow her lips hijacked her and it just kept going and going.

What happened to the bouquet she didn't know. All she knew was that Will's hands were suddenly pulling her closer to him, exploring the bare skin of her shoulders and playing with the loose tendrils of hair at the base of her neck.

Someone broke it off—she wasn't sure who—and she found herself staring at him.

'What…what was that for?' he said.

The old reflex to hide every genuine desire behind a guise of something flippant and outrageous surfaced. He'd kissed her unexpectedly in the orchard, hadn't he?

'That,' she said, pulling out of his grasp and smiling cheekily at him, 'makes us even.'

Josie found Hattie sitting on her mother's lap eating a strawberry. From the trail of watery red juice down her chin, she guessed it wasn't the first.

'Come on, poppet. Time to go home and get changed for bed.'

'I wanted to dance with Will again.'

Josie wiped her daughter's face with a paper napkin. 'It's already a little past your bedtime and you look tired.'

'I'm not,' Hattie said, ending the sentence with a yawn.

'Come on.'

She held out a hand and Hattie reluctantly slid off her grandmother's lap and placed her hand in Josie's.

'Run and say goodnight to Grandpa, will you, darling?' her mother said. 'He'll be terribly upset if you don't.'

Hattie nodded and ran off to the other side of the marquee.

'Don't look at me like that, Mum. I know I'm lucky and she does everything I ask her without much fuss. Unlike me, of course.'

'You always were so strong-willed, Josephine. I never could understand why there was such a great need to test the boundaries.'

Josie took a deep breath. She wasn't quite sure where the urge had come from herself. Rules, boundaries—whatever you liked to call them—meant total freedom was ruled out. Only certain choices were available and she wanted the chance to do it all, live it all, not look back in her old age at years wasted stagnating while her heart ached for more.

'Never mind.' Her mother wiped her hands on a serviette and stood up, straightening the jacket of her *eau-de-nil* Chanel suit as she did so. She gave Josie the oddest of smiles, followed by—wait for it—a wink. 'You seem to be turning it all to your advantage in the end.'

Josie put a hand on one hip and frowned. 'What's that supposed to mean?'

Her mother leant in close to whisper loudly in her ear. 'Just that I think you're being very resourceful in areas other than cake-decorating. He's quite a catch.' She stepped back and patted Josie on the arm.

'You saw us?'

Her mother raised an eyebrow.

'It's not…I mean, there's nothing… Mum, will you stop looking at me like that?'

'I just wanted you to know that you have my blessing. I was starting to worry you'd find a suitable man at all.'

Josie shifted her weight so the burning pain from the blister on her left heel switched to her right one. 'I don't need a man, Mum. I'm OK on my own. And who were you supposing I was going to hook up with anyway?'

Her mother wrinkled her nose.

'Oh, I see. You were expecting me to continue my fall from grace and end up shacked up in a squat with a bloke named *Spud.*'

'Don't be ridiculous.'

Josie held out her hand to Hattie, who was skipping back towards them. 'Well, thanks for the vote of confidence, Mum.'

She walked away without turning back, pulling Hattie along with her. Then she felt a gentle tugging on her hand. 'Mummy? I didn't say night-night to Grandma.'

'Sorry, sweetheart. You run back and give her a kiss. I'll wait right here.'

She didn't turn round to watch Hattie go, knowing that if she looked at her mother at this precise second she would probably blow her top. Just as she'd thought her parents might value her as a unique individual in her own right, it turned out they were only impressed with her if she managed to marry her way into respectability and rest on her husband's laurels. They didn't know her at all.

And anyway, whoever said she was thinking of getting involved with Will, let alone marrying him?

Oh, come on! a little voice inside her head exclaimed. *Who are you kidding? You're terminally attracted to him. What's more, you might even be half in love with him.*

'I am not!' she said out loud then looked around to see if anyone had heard. He's boring and stuffy and…

She didn't have the heart to continue lecturing herself. Even the awkward half of her knew the words were hollow.

She heard Hattie's footsteps on the cobbles of the courtyard and turned to hold her hand again.

'I'm tired, Mummy, from all the running. Can you carry me?'

Josie couldn't resist Hattie when she pulled that puppy-dog look.

'Oh, all right, then. But you have to promise not to wriggle. These dresses are slippery and I'll only drop you.'

Hattie nodded and jumped up, tucking her legs round Josie's back and clinging on to her neck.

'My goodness, Hattie! How much of that cake did you eat? You weigh an absolute ton.'

Will's voice came from somewhere over her shoulder. 'Here. Let me.'

Josie gave him a thin smile. 'No, I'm fine on my own. You go and enjoy the party.'

She hobbled forward a few steps, suddenly very aware of the blisters on her feet again. Carrying Hattie seemed to double the pain.

A strong pair of arms reached for Hattie and the little traitor practically jumped into them. She gave Will a look that she hoped would shrivel him to the size of a pea, only to find him grinning good-naturedly at her.

'It won't work, you know.'

'Fine. I give up.'

She set off at the briskest pace her screaming feet would allow. 'Oh, for goodness' sake! Who cares any more?' she fumed and kicked the stilettos off her feet and into the nearest bush.

The way to the cottage was paved with ancient stone slabs and they felt like cool slices of heaven as she walked, even with the burning pain in the balls of her feet now they'd been allowed to flatten out again.

Will shifted Hattie to a more comfortable position. Her head was resting on his broad shoulder and her eyelids were drooping. Josie reached up and stroked her daughter's hair. Her eyes locked with Will's.

She knew what he wanted to say. *What was all that about back there—the kiss? Where is this going?*

They were questions she desperately wanted to know the answers to herself, but knew she had no more of a clue than he did.

Hattie's body seemed to get denser as he walked and, without craning his neck to check, he knew she was in the dozy half-state between wakefulness and sleep. When they finally reached the cottage he handed her over to Josie, who was steadily avoiding eye contact, and watched as she carried her up the stairs to bed.

One of the guides had agreed to babysit so Josie could enjoy the rest of the party and make sure the band was paid and the clearing-up operation began smoothly.

Will rested against the wall beside the front door. She wasn't getting rid of him that easily. One moment she was full of fun and passion, the next she was giving him a blast of icy air. He needed to know where he stood.

Ten minutes later she descended the narrow stairs, still wearing the floor-length gown. She didn't look at all surprised he was still standing there. She didn't exactly look overjoyed, either.

'I have to go and find my shoes.'

He nodded and followed her down the garden path and back to the spot where she'd tossed them away.

'I know it's stupid,' she said while rummaging through the base of a bush, 'but I can't bring myself to waste things any more, even if they are instruments of torture.'

He smiled. 'Were you accustomed to "wasting" shoes in the past, then?'

'A-ha!' She pulled a dark reddish-pink shoe from the herbaceous border and gave him a triumphant look. 'Oh, yes. I can't remember how many pairs of designer shoes I abandoned after a night out on the town because they were giving me grief. The tramps in London must have thought the Prada fairy visited on a regular basis.'

The sky was now a dusky lavender on one horizon and a deep, hypnotic blue on the other, making it harder to distinguish red tones from greens. He dropped the branch he was holding and tried another bush. Something smooth and satiny was hidden among the fronds of a fern. He picked it out and handed it to her.

'Thanks. I think.'

She looked wistfully along the path to where they could just see a corner of the marquee.

'You don't want to go back up there, do you?'

She looked at the ground then shook her head. 'I've had enough. Enough of all the small talk, the mind-numbing social climbing. I've had enough of this—' She prodded her corset-like bodice with a finger. Then she looked at the shoes, one in each hand. 'I've definitely had enough of these.'

Her arm muscles twitched in preparation and he reached forward and tugged the shoes out of her hands.

'Perhaps I'd better hang on to them. I don't want to spend all night hunting through the shrubbery.'

She sighed. 'I'm going to have to put them back on again sooner or later.'

'Why?'

'Well, we've got to be there. Just in case.'

He shook his head. 'They can manage without us for a bit. Let's play hookey.'

She grabbed the shoes back off him. 'Play hookey?'

'You know. Play truant. Bunk off.'

'I know what it means, Will. I practically invented the concept. At my school they used to call it "doing a Josie"!'

'Then you're familiar with the procedure. Good. This is going to be easier than I thought.' Before she could argue, he took her by the hand and tugged her in the direction of an opening in the hedge.

The stars were just beginning to sparkle in the darkening sky. Every few minutes a new one would appear, as if waking energised from a long slumber.

Josie sat beside Will on the grassy lawn of one of the smaller 'rooms' hidden away in the maze-like gardens. Each area had its own particular atmosphere and function.

This garden had been designed as an open-air theatre, with a grassy raised stage on one side and a gentle crescent-shaped slope for the select audience to sit on. At most, it would have seated thirty or forty people comfortably.

'My feet are killing me.'

They were sitting on the slope facing the 'stage'. Her knees were bent and her feet flat on the ground and she raised her skirts to look at them, not that she expected it to help at all.

Will, who was mirroring her pose, stopped staring straight ahead and looked at them too. She watched, transfixed and unable to move, as he reached down and picked up her right foot and took it in his hands. It became unusually hard to breathe.

He seemed to be holding her small, arched foot as if it were a glass slipper, something precious and delicate. His large hands felt warm and comforting as he stroked and kneaded the sole of her foot. Pretty soon her awkwardness melted away and she was feeling soothed and relaxed.

He didn't speak. He didn't even look at her. All his attention was focused on her foot. And it felt unbelievable. Sensuous. Intimate.

Words would only have spoiled whatever was building between them and she didn't want to break the spell.

He placed her bare foot down gently on the grass and picked up the other one. She wasn't sure she could take much more of this. It was too much and yet it wasn't enough. She let herself fall backwards until the grassy slope supported her, and closed her eyes.

What did this mean?

Will seemed in no hurry to give her any answers. Slowly, methodically, he massaged out the knots and kinks produced by endless hours in high heels. He applied the same kind of deft concentration to the task that she'd seen before. Every stroke, every touch was economical, hitting exactly the right spots, never pinching, never hurting.

On the outside her muscles were slowly melting like a pool of butter, but deep, deep inside she started to shake.

When Will finally finished, she couldn't decide whether she was relieved or disappointed. He stroked the last piece of tension from the arch of her foot and placed it down gently on the grass next to her other one.

She didn't dare turn and look at him, but she knew what he was doing. He lay down beside her, so close they were almost touching, and for what seemed like an age they listened to the sound of each other's breathing and watched the stars emerge.

She wanted to say something—something glib and funny. Something about liking his version of playing hookey better than her own. It certainly got one in a lot less trouble—or maybe it was just a different kind of trouble.

Anyway, her lips seemed to be glued shut.

Whatever wordless communication was arcing between them was enough, deeper and more profound than anything her brain could conjure up with mere sounds and syllables.

Her nerve-endings burned and sang as she felt his strong, capable fingers reach between her own. She held her breath. She'd done her share of wild things in the past, had her flings and more serious boyfriends. But no moment with any of them, not even Miles, had made her feel so alive or so terrified.

They were only holding hands, yet she felt as if her whole body had been turned inside out, as if she were wearing her soul on the outside. It felt raw. Too much. She'd never realised that true freedom could be this dangerous. She wasn't sure she liked it.

Her mother approved of Will, and twenty minutes ago she'd been tempted to do what she always did when her mother encouraged her to do something— the exact opposite.

In this case, it was actually the sensible thing to do. If she followed her mother's wishes to the logical conclusion, it would be disastrous. He wasn't for her; she didn't want his life. If she married him, she'd be condemned to an endless string of days like today. And so would Hattie.

And while her brain was ticking off all the sensible reasons to get up and walk away, the rest of her was staging some kind of mutiny. In this moment, all those reasons why they were so totally wrong for each other ebbed away and she was left with the cold grass against her back, the breeze on her face and Will's warm hand joined with her own.

Her heart jumped up a gear.

She started to turn her head towards him, hesitated, and carried on. He must have heard the movement because, a fraction of a second later, he did the same thing and then they were joined, not just at the finger-tips, but also soul to soul as she stared deep into his perfect eyes.

The air around them crackled with static, so strong she was sure her hair must be fluffed up and standing on end.

The way he was looking at her…

He didn't care. He knew all the logical objections and he didn't care. He knew her past, that she'd been labelled a rebel, a failure and a troublemaker, and still he was looking at her as if he wanted to disappear inside her.

All the crackles in the atmosphere around them seemed to gather together and charge the air, like the interior of a storm cloud just before it released a lightning bolt.

And then she felt it.

Zap. Tingles all the way down her body.

He *got* her.

He'd found what he'd been searching for. And not from gaining a title, respect or succeeding in business. All those things had been blind alleys. Stupidly, he'd thought they were the path to happiness, the path to belonging.

None of that mattered now. His business could go under, the Radcliffes could steal his land, prove him illegitimate and snatch the title and he still wouldn't swap any of it for this moment.

Looking into her eyes like this, he felt all the peripheral stuff melt away. He forgot about the pink hair, the self-protective sassy attitude, the outrageous mouth that got her into trouble. All he could see was the passion, the ingenuity, the ability to dig deep and reach out.

And he loved what he saw.

She reached her free hand up, rolling towards him as she did so, and ever so gently stroked the side of his face. He wanted to close his eyes, heighten the sensation of her soft fingers on his cheek by cutting out all other stimuli, but somehow he couldn't. He needed to see those bottomless eyes. The tenderness in them almost brought tears to his own.

He wasn't sure who moved first, but soon their lips brushed against each other. He could feel her breath mingling with his as she pulled back only a hair's-breadth.

The kisses they'd shared before had been pure impulse. A moment when instinct and some deeper desire had taken over and all he'd been aware of was the intoxicating physical sensation of her lips against his.

The kiss that followed was so, so different. He knew exactly what he was doing, exactly whom he was kissing. Today, for the first time, he'd seen her. All of her layers of armour had been invisible to him and now he couldn't help seeing her that way. He always would.

And he knew exactly what he was feeling. He loved her.

He wanted to be able to think of all sorts of flowery phrases from the love songs he knew, but they were too complicated, too fussy. He loved her. It was as simple and as complicated as that.

He pulled her closer to him, held her, touched her. The sky was darkening above them, he could sense it without even opening his eyes, and all he wanted at this moment was to stay here, frozen in time, never leaving this perfect moment.

'Josie,' he whispered, leaving her mouth and kissing down the side of her jaw.

She eased back, looked at him. Her face was full of awe and full of questions. For once that runaway mouth had stalled. He smiled gently and kissed it again.

Then there was noise and a sudden flash above them.

They broke apart and he was forced to look away from her.

Josie squealed and scrambled to her feet. 'Jeff! I'm going to kill him! He just took a photo of us… like that.'

His eyes were still stinging from the brightness of the flashbulb. Orange and purple blobs obscured his field of vision. Fabric rustled beside him. Josie was on the move.

He reached for her and caught hold of her arm. 'Josie, wait!'

She tried to pull away. 'No, Will. We've got to find him. We've got to stop him.'

'Is it really so awful? It's only one photograph.'

She turned to face him but kept moving in the direction of the gap in the hedge, her feet treading backwards. 'You don't understand,' she said, shaking her head. 'It will mess everything up! You don't want this kind of publicity.'

She was crying now. 'I'm so sorry, Will. I'm so sorry. It was all my idea.'

With that she turned and ran out of the secluded garden.

Will didn't waste a moment following her. He

caught up with her almost immediately. His legs were infinitely longer and she was struggling with her dress and her bare feet on the flagstones.

'Josie!' He pulled her close to him. She was shaking. 'You can't give chase dressed like that. Go back to the cottage and put some shoes on at least. Please?' She nodded against his chest. He kissed the top of her head, framed her face with both his hands and made her look at him. 'It'll be OK, I promise.'

And then he was gone, racing up the path towards the marquee.

He wasn't going to let anyone hurt Josie. She might pretend that she didn't care what people thought, but he'd seen her expression when Piers had brought up that other photograph at dinner. He never wanted to see that look of pain and humiliation on her face again. With amazing courage, she'd turned her life around and become a success and he wasn't going to let one photograph destroy all of that.

There was no sign of Jeff in the marquee, only couples slow-dancing to the mellow jazz sounds. Will checked in the cloakrooms and the food-preparation areas just in case. Nothing.

He was out of breath now and stopped jogging, slowing to a brisk walk. The rat had to be around here somewhere. He circled the house, which took him a good ten minutes. The only option left was to search the gardens. He jogged down the steps from the top lawn into the rose garden.

Everything was quiet. He walked the perimeter of

the garden, keeping his footsteps quiet and straining his ears. Still nothing.

A shadow passed from the rose garden into the herb garden. Will started to follow it but stopped almost instantly. He could hear a low voice muttering in a one-sided conversation. He crept up to the hedge and listened.

'No, mate. I'm telling you, I struck gold again. I did the wedding photographs and was about to pack up and go home when I stumbled on something very interesting. *Celebrity Life* won't take it. It's not their sort of thing, but I knew you'd be interested.'

There was a pause. 'Yeah. Yeah… I'll e-mail it through to you as soon as possible. Only I've got to find my way out of these gardens first. It's like a blooming maze.'

Will smiled. He knew exactly where Jeff was—in the Mediterranean garden. There were two exits but he guessed Jeff wouldn't take the one he'd just used. He changed direction, went back into the rose garden and exited again down a narrow path lined with statues that led to where the photographer was. He could hear him now, speaking into his phone as he neared the arch in the hedge.

Will ducked behind a statue and waited. A few seconds later Jeff appeared, the light of his mobile phone giving him away. Will reached forward and snatched it out of his hand.

'I think I'll have that, thank you.'

Jeff stumbled backwards and swore.

'You were hired to do a particular job,' Will said. 'And that did not include trespassing in my gardens and invading my privacy.'

Jeff grinned at him. 'The brief said "formal wedding photographs and informal shots at the reception". I think you were getting pretty informal back there, don't you?'

For the first time in his life, Will was seriously tempted to punch someone on the nose. Then he thought of Josie and how thumping this man would only antagonise him and push him into hurting her even more.

'Is there anything I can do to convince you not to sell that photograph?'

'Not a lot. It's going to be a nice little earner for me. *Buzz Magazine* will easily give me five grand for it.'

Will would have offered him ten if he'd had it in his bank account. Unfortunately, everything he had was ploughed into Elmhurst at this point and he didn't think spare change was going to do the trick.

'What if I offer you something better?'

Jeff shrugged. 'It would have to be good.'

'We are opening an exhibition here in two weeks' time. How about exclusive coverage for *Celebrity Life* magazine?'

Jeff grimaced and shook his head. 'Maybe. If the shot I'd got had been less...interesting, I would probably have taken you up on that.'

The urge to punch him returned. Will looked around him, desperately searching the air for answers, and then it hit him. He looked Jeff straight in the eye.

'OK. How about this for an exclusive...?'

CHAPTER THIRTEEN

FOR once in her life Josie didn't know what to wear. She stood in front of her wardrobe, the doors flung wide, and looked at the row of clothes.

Normally, she just picked whatever stood out to her the most. But today, she really didn't want to wear the psychedelic T-shirt that had caught her eye first. It seemed too loud, too brash.

Eventually, she took her one plain T-shirt out of her drawer and pulled it over her head. It was the only un-adorned T-shirt she owned. Most of her clothes seem to scream *look at me* or *notice me*, as if she were waving a giant banner to the world.

But today there was only one person's attention she wanted. And she'd already discovered that, where he was concerned, she didn't need to shout.

'Are you ready, Hattie?' she yelled.

A little face appeared around her bedroom door and nodded.

Josie grinned. 'This time I get to be the princess and you get to be the troll, OK?'

Hattie shook her head.

'Oh, well, I'd better start making myself ugly again, then.' She pulled a face and Hattie squealed. Josie laughed and turned to face the mirror. Not a trace of make-up was on her face. She looked fresh and—oh, my goodness!—she was even glowing.

The only cloud on the distant horizon was that rat, Jeff. She'd changed her clothes and had run after him last night, but he'd been nowhere to be seen. She'd checked the lane beside the church where he'd parked his car. It had been empty.

She hoped Will had found him. She hadn't seen him since. By the time she'd jogged back from the church it had been five to eleven and time to relieve the baby-sitter.

She closed her eyes. Please, don't let this all be a dream.

It was a crisp and bright, perfect Sunday morning. She held hands with Hattie as they walked through the gardens. A small team of people were still clearing up and taking down the marquee.

It seemed that, after last night, every part of the garden was imprinted with memories of Will. There was the spot where they'd watched the bridal car leave—where she'd kissed him. On the top lawn, she could only remember the time spent waltzing in his arms. And when they passed the entrance to the outdoor theatre, she got goose-pimples.

In the rose garden, staring into the fountain, there was a figure. For a split-second her heart lurched, but then she realised it was a woman, slim but obviously in her golden years. Her hair was a pale platinum blonde and she wore a smart brown suit finished off with leopard-print shoes.

Josie walked up to her as Hattie skipped around the flower beds on the narrow paths, singing to herself. She kept her voice low, so as not to startle the woman. 'Good morning. You must be Ruby.' She held out her hand.

The woman turned, a hint of sadness in her eyes. 'How did you know?'

'I'm Josie. I'm Will's…' She couldn't come up with a definition. 'I work with Will. He's told me a lot about you.'

Ruby smiled and shook Josie's hand. 'I'm very pleased to meet you too.'

Ruby looked up from the fountain and took in the view of the gardens and Elmhurst Hall.

'It seems strange to be here after all these years. I knew the previous lord when I was younger.'

Josie just raised her eyebrows. It didn't seem right to tell Ruby she knew anything about her private life.

'He had a bit of a thing for me.' She gave a weak smile. 'And for a while, I was a little dazzled, believing I could be a grand lady and live in a posh house. I really thought he was going to propose at one point, but he never did. Perhaps I was just being silly.' Her voice trailed off and got very quiet. 'It was just as well he never did.'

For a few seconds, she just stared at the hall.

'It wasn't meant to be. He introduced me to his

brother—Will's grandfather—and, well, that was that. Bang. Love at first sight. We were married inside two months and I never regretted it.'

Her eyes shimmered.

'It's a little strange to be here now for the first time. I can see what my William gave up for me and it makes me sad. And I can see why I wasn't good enough for Harry. I don't belong in a place like this.'

At that point Hattie ran up and stared at Ruby. 'Hello. Are you going to be the fairy godmother?'

'Ruby, meet my daughter, Hattie. She's five and she thinks the whole world is a fairy tale.'

Ruby smiled at Hattie, her sadness forgotten. 'You know, I think I will.'

'Why don't you run off and hide, poppet? The fairy godmother and I will count to one hundred. How about that?'

Ruby and Josie turned their backs and counted silently while Hattie skipped off.

Josie looked down at their feet side by side as she silently mouthed the numbers. 'I've been known to wear a bit of animal print myself,' she said.

What on earth was his grandmother up to now? Will watched from the window as she skipped around the rose garden, twirling as she went. Then he spotted Hattie, flitting along like a fairy princess, and it all became clear.

A few seconds later Josie appeared, stomping her feet and waving her arms about madly.

His heart swelled so much he thought it would burst. She looked just as stunning this morning in a plain T-shirt and jeans as she had yesterday in her bridesmaid's dress. The shoulder-length brown hair swung to and fro as she chased Hattie, snarling and gnashing her teeth. She was beautiful.

He should have known that Nan and Josie would get on like a house on fire.

He turned away from the window and leant against the sill.

Josie was *his* Ruby.

He could do as the previous Lord Radcliffe had done and choose honour and the family reputation— and regret it for the rest of his life—or he could follow in his grandfather's footsteps and choose love, letting everything else slide down the pan.

He looked at the family crest above the fireplace. Beatrice had said he was a commoner and would drag the family reputation into the mud again.

He so badly wanted to prove her wrong.

He was jogging down the steps from the top lawn to meet them. Josie stopped growling at Hattie and her heart gave a little skip. At present, he was watching his feet as he descended the steps but halfway down he raised his eyes and they locked gazes.

Her stomach bottomed out.

Hattie was tugging her arm and trying to drag her off for another game, but she couldn't move. All she could do was watch Will coming closer and closer.

'Hi,' he said.

'Hi,' she said back.

Ruby, who had just twirled into range, stopped and looked at them. 'I think it's high time Hattie gave me a tour of the gardens. Come on, Hattie.' She looked from Will to Josie again then disappeared.

Still neither of them said anything. Josie's tummy fluttered. If she knew Will, he was going to come out with something incredibly formal and starchy. It was what he always did when he was nervous.

Instead he took her by surprise, sweeping her into his arms and kissing her. Oh, my...

Nothing starchy about that.

Once he'd started, it was as if he couldn't stop. He kissed her mouth, her ears, her eyelids, and then he moved down to her neck... Josie stopped counting body parts. In fact, she stopped thinking altogether.

Finally, they broke apart and he looked at her. It was that same look he'd given her last night. Her knees went all tingly.

He took her hand and they walked silently round the garden, not needing words, just needing each other. As they reached the arch that led into the herb garden he stopped and turned to face her.

She read what he was going to say in his eyes before the words left his lips.

'I love you.'

So simple. No frills, no grandiose gestures. It was so Will. Suddenly, she understood the beauty of understatement. Previously, she would have thought her reaction to hearing those words would have sent her leaping and whooping around the gardens, but instead, she reached up and touched his face, exploring his cheeks with her fingertips.

She swallowed. A single tear edged its way over her lashes and plopped onto her cheek. 'I love you too.'

Will picked her up as easily as if she were a feather, crushing her to him and let out a loud cheer. Then he swung her round and round until her feet flew outwards and they both felt sick and dizzy.

Finally, he lowered her until her feet touched the ground as they clung on to each other, too scared to let go in case they fell into a heap.

Will whispered in her ear. 'I had such great plans to do this all properly.'

Her voice was clogged with tears. 'No, that was perfect.'

He laughed and kissed her again. 'At least let me do the next bit the way I'd planned.'

The next bit? Her heart started hammering inside her chest.

Will let go of her and stood back apace. 'Josie, I would very much like to take you out to dinner tonight.'

She took a deep breath. Of course Will wouldn't jump the gun. First things first. Everything in its proper order. But for a moment there, she had thought he was going to ask a different question…

He looked so proper standing there, his hands clasped in front of him and a hopeful look on his face. She giggled and, for the very first time in her life, she curtsied without being forced to. 'I would be honoured to go to dinner with you, Lord Radcliffe.'

'No,' he said, pulling her to him. 'None of that. We're just Josie and Will, remember? That's all that matters.'

She looked up at him. 'What about Jeff? The photograph? Did you manage to catch up with him?'

He hugged her tight and placed his chin on top of her head. 'It doesn't matter. Don't worry about it.'

The sound of rustling paper made him pause as he walked past Josie's office. She was flicking through a tabloid newspaper, hardly spending enough time on each page to register the headlines. A stack of papers and celebrity magazines sat on the desk in front of her. He knew what she was looking for.

She got to the end of the paper and folded it shut. Lines appeared between her brows.

The photograph wasn't in there, and she wasn't going to find it in the rest of the stack either.

He carried on walking and entered his own office. Once seated behind the desk, he rested his chin on his fist. Jeff had given him two weeks to come up with the exclusive he'd promised him. Five days had already passed and the ticking clock in his brain was starting to mar the joy he was feeling at being with Josie.

He knew what he wanted. He wanted her to be his wife.

But things were never simple. He was asking her to give up a lot for him and, although he didn't doubt the strength of her feelings, it was a big step to ask her to take in such a short time. She hated her title, and here he was about to ask her to adopt the life she'd so vehemently rejected.

He'd suggested they keep their relationship a secret, just for a few weeks. He'd wanted to give her time to get used to the idea of them being together before they went public and the rest of the world chipped in with its opinion.

If only he could make her see that they could make their own rules, live their own lives. For heaven's sake, there had been much, much bigger scandals in the history of England than a minor nobleman marrying a pink-haired socialite. Some of the things he'd read in the history books were shocking even by today's standards.

All his life he'd tried to fit in, live by tradition. Marrying Josie would break the mould, but he knew that beyond anything he wanted a life with her and Hattie and he was prepared to do anything, create whole new traditions, to make that possible.

Nine days. That was all the time he had left to help her take the blinkers off and see the future for what it could be. What if it wasn't enough?

The Saturday after next was the opening of Harry's exhibition. There had been even more Press interest than they'd anticipated and a couple of the London papers wanted to do colour supplements in their Sunday magazines. One was even going to run a feature on Harry's life.

The figures his accountant had given him looked

good. If the exhibition did as well as expected and the wedding bookings came in for next year, Elmhurst would be saved. But it wouldn't mean anything if Josie weren't by his side.

And, in a few years, when all the debts were paid off, it would become a thriving business, helping the community and strengthening the local economy.

Josie and he could be so happy together. He had to make her see.

He had it all planned out. The ring was locked in the bureau drawer in the study, the key hidden back on top of the bookcase. On the night of the reception to celebrate the opening of the exhibition, he was going to stand in the Great Hall here at Elmhurst and tell the world that he loved Josie Harrington-Jones and ask her to be his wife.

Josie was filing a stack of papers away in Will's office when she heard the answerphone beep into life. At first, she didn't stop what she was doing.

'Lord Radcliffe, about the little matter we discussed the other night… I just want you to know that I'm still sitting on that photograph, although the editor of *Buzz Magazine* is spitting mad about it. We've got a deal, don't you worry.' Jeff paused. 'And just so you know, mate, she's not going to be in disgrace this time.'

Josie dropped the papers she was holding into any old slot in the filing cabinet and walked across the room to the desk. She jabbed the button on the base unit of the phone to play the message back again.

No, she'd heard it right first time.

A disgrace? Will didn't want the photograph to get out because he thought she was a disgrace?

She took a deep breath, trying to control the shaking in her limbs. She was so angry she could rip his head off. And perhaps that was a *really* good idea. She knew exactly where he was; he was up in the newly refurbished attics, checking on the finishing touches to the exhibition.

Despite her little legs, it only took a few minutes for her to get up there. She found Will staring at the suit of Japanese armour. He turned and smiled as she walked towards him. 'It looks even better all cleaned up and polished, doesn't it?'

And then he noticed the look on her face and he went all serious. 'Josie, what's wrong?'

'Is there something you want to tell me, Will? A little secret you've been keeping from me?'

He hesitated, and she knew before he even opened his mouth that he was about to lie to her. He didn't do deception well. Up until just now, she'd have said he didn't do it at all, but she'd obviously been wrong.

'No, I don't think so.'

'You're lying to me. You've made some deal with that bastard photographer. Don't bother to deny it. He left a message on your answerphone. It was very enlightening.'

Will walked towards her and took her hands in his. She snatched them away again.

'For the last ten days I've lived in fear, waiting to

see that photograph in one of the celebrity rags. And all this time you didn't think to tell me that you'd managed to stop him?'

He stepped towards her and she backed away. 'Josie! You don't understand.'

'Oh, I understand rather too well. You don't trust me, and more than that, you're ashamed of me. You don't want people to know that we're together.'

'No! No, that's not true!'

'Then why keep this from me?'

This time Will took a step backwards. 'I want to explain, but I can't. Not yet.'

Her lip desperately wanted to quiver, but she wasn't going to let it. She wasn't going to show him how his lack of faith in her cut her heart in two. He was just like all the rest. He wanted her to be something she wasn't and, although she loved him dearly, she couldn't be the person he wanted her to be.

'You're not fit to stand up here and look at Harry's things! He was a man with heart, a man who knew what was important in life. You! You only care about your stupid family, your reputation and being accepted by slime like the Beauforts.'

He was across the room, trying to pull her into his arms. 'No, Josie. I love you. You don't understand.'

She pushed him away. 'Well, I'm making it really easy for you. I'm taking myself out of the equation. You'll have no risk of disgrace.'

'You're leaving? Now?'

'I'll stay until the exhibition opens. I'll see this

through because of Harry, not because of you. I owe it to him. After that, Hattie and I will be gone.'

If she weren't so angry, the look of panic on his face would have broken her heart. 'OK, you say you love me and you're not ashamed of me. Prove it! Go downstairs, ring up a tabloid paper—you can pick which one—and tell them we are going to be together.'

Will started. 'Please, Josie. I wish I could explain, but I can't. I need more time.'

There. He couldn't do it. She was OK to mess around with, but not good enough to marry. It was better to leave now, before she fell even more in love with him.

She swallowed a lump of tears, turned and ran down the staircase, out of the hall and all the way through the gardens to her cottage.

Once up in her bedroom, she took a good look in her full-length mirror. She hardly recognised herself. Who was this woman with neat, mousy-brown hair? These clothes didn't belong to her. She shouldn't be wearing a crisp white blouse, a skirt and heels.

She'd done this for him, without even realising it. And he'd fallen in love with the illusion, rather than the real Josie Harrington-Jones. For a week or two the fairy godmother might have waved her magic wand and turned her into a princess, but underneath she was still the same old troll.

She scrabbled to undo the buttons of the blouse, slipped off the skirt and kicked her heels across the room. Once in her underwear she felt better. She picked up the clothes, bundled them into her arms and took them into the bathroom, where she stuffed them in the bin.

As she stood up, her eyes fell on a box in the open bathroom cabinet.

It was time to reclaim her identity.

Will sat in Harry's old study, counting the seconds. The little drawer in the bureau was open and a small velvet box sat on the desk in front of him. He'd had to let her go. Words just weren't enough when Josie got all fired up like that.

He couldn't have done what she'd asked and leaked the story of their relationship to the Press. The very thing he'd wanted to do by striking a deal with the photographer was to save her from more pain, and if he didn't give Jeff the exclusive pictures of their engagement there'd be more pictures of her in the paper labelled *Lady Go-Go* and all the hard work she'd done in the last few years would have been for nothing.

He closed the little box and put it back in the drawer but didn't lock it. Hopefully, he'd be needing it soon.

It had been two hours and forty-nine minutes since she'd marched out of the attic and disappeared. Perhaps that was long enough for her to cool down and listen. He checked the second hand on his watch. He'd wait until it was three hours. Then he'd go.

Exactly eleven minutes later, he started his search. Surprisingly, he found her sitting at her desk, quietly working away on her computer. But appearances could be very deceptive.

Her hair was the brightest, loudest fire-engine red he'd ever seen.

It was a message to him. What had she said about redheads being as hot as a Vindaloo? He was in deep, deep trouble.

Words definitely weren't going to be enough.

The Great Hall looked fabulous. Josie walked around, chatting to caterers and making sure all the arrangements were finalised for a big reception after the unveiling of the exhibition.

When she'd finished she climbed slowly up the stairs to the Long Gallery then continued up to the attic. The space up here was completely transformed. Gone were the dust and cobwebs and, in their place, polished floorboards and crystal-clean windows. Ropes on stands were laid out to guide people round the exhibition.

She followed the route, taking it all in. Crowds of people would be up here later on, marvelling at Harry's collection, but she'd wanted to come up while it was still empty. It would be the last time she'd see all of these wonderful things.

A gentle smile curved her lips. Harry would have been thrilled.

At least she'd—no, they'd—accomplished this before she'd had to leave. She and Will together. Funny how she'd already started thinking of them as a partnership, even before she'd fallen in love with him.

She'd hardly seen him at all in the last few days. The thought made her breath catch. After her ultimatum, some small part of her had wanted him to kick up a fuss, to fight for her. Instead, he'd been almost invisible.

She'd been right after all. He'd had second thoughts but, Will being Will, he couldn't bring himself to do the ungentlemanly thing and break it off.

She wandered from room to room. The items in Harry's collection had been grouped together so the five rooms now housed Oriental craftsmanship, old-fashioned toys, musical instruments, maritime objects and old bikes and prams. Masks and carvings adorned the walls of the corridors. The whole exhibition was even better than she'd imagined when Will had come up with the idea.

Will. Did every train of thought have to end up at that destination?

She took the stairs back down to the Great Hall and had one last look around. She'd had enough of memories. It was time to get out of the hall and into the gardens. She was pretty sure there wouldn't be much fresh air and freedom when she moved back home to her parents' tomorrow. Even with her pay rise she couldn't afford to do anything else.

She walked out of the arched doorway and onto the top lawn. The weather was starting to turn cold again and, as she stood on the grass overlooking the rose garden, she shivered and rubbed her arms.

Someone was walking on the path down there. It looked like Will, but he was wearing something strange on his head. She squinted at the multicoloured blob, trying to work out what it was.

Oh, my goodness! It was the hat she'd made him back in the spring, only she'd never seen him wear it before today.

'Will!'

He turned briefly, registered who had called out to him and hurried away.

Quickly, she hurried down the stone steps into the rose garden. Why was he running away from her? Was he really that desperate to see the back of her? By the time she was down amongst the flower beds, Will had vanished. She jogged down the path and decided to search for him. Something wasn't right here.

He wasn't in the Mediterranean garden, the herb garden or near the fish pond. On a hunch she tried the orchard. Ever since that night when he'd kissed her in the darkness she'd felt drawn to it. Maybe he felt the same unconscious pull.

It seemed to take hours to get there. Her heart drummed a double beat for every step she took. At last she reached the entrance. The squat trees were covered in waxy green leaves and on every branch was the promise of fruit. Sweet fruit that she would never have the chance to savour. The thought brought tears to her eyes.

And there, sitting on the bench in the corner, staring

into space, was the man who'd brought such sweetness and such bitterness into her life in the space of just a fortnight.

'Will?'

He jumped to his feet at her voice. 'Josie!'

She walked towards him and tried desperately not to let the emotion show in her movements, her voice. 'Are you avoiding me?'

He pulled the hat down as far over his ears as it would go. He looked embarrassed. Up until now she'd harboured a secret hope that she hardly dared acknowledge, even to herself. She wanted him to come to her, to tell her she was wrong, that he loved her just the way she was and could never be ashamed of her.

His body language sent her hope plummeting like a stone. He couldn't even stand to be within ten feet of her any more.

'I just… I'll talk to you later—at the reception.'

He started half-walking, half-running away from her, aiming for one of the other exits. She ran after him. She had to know once and for all. Her voice broke and the shout came out as a hoarse squeak. 'Will!'

He turned round but still kept walking backwards, trying to increase the distance between them. 'I want to talk to you, Josie. I really do. But it will have to wait until the reception. You'll understand later.'

She wanted to understand now!

'You're wearing my hat,' she said, mainly out of desperation.

Something of hers. Something very un-Will.

'I know.' Will touched his head, his fingers feeling the bumps of the crocheted hat's stripes. He was worried about something. The knowledge made her jittery.

She couldn't think. All she could do was stare at that stupid hat. Which was a piece of poor craftsmanship, if ever she'd seen one. There was an unfinished end, a piece of pink fluff sticking out on one side.

Instinctively, her fingers reached for it. 'You've got something on your…'

Her skin made contact with the fluff and instantly she pulled her hand back and pressed her fingers against her lips. Will looked guiltily at her.

No! No, he hadn't! That stupid, wonderful man…

She reached out again, tears filling her eyes, and stroked the skin of his cheek above his temple, her fingers dipping under the edge of the hat. 'Oh, Will.' Her voice was husky. 'What have you done to yourself?'

Her chin wobbled. She grasped the brim of the hat between her thumb and forefinger and tugged it gently. It fell into her hand.

Will wore the expression of a naughty schoolboy. She didn't know whether to laugh or cry.

'Your hair!' she hiccuped. 'Your beautiful dark hair. It's—'

'Hot-Pants Pink,' he finished for her.

And then she was crying, and kissing him all over his face, even though she didn't know why she was doing either.

'You can't go to the reception like this! What were you thinking?'

He pulled her into his arms and held her tight against his chest. 'I did it for you,' he said, his voice gravelly with emotion. 'To show you that I love you and I am *not* ashamed of you and I would do anything to make you see that. I was going to stand up there in front of all those people and ask you to be my wife. We're in this together, you and me.'

She broke down in uncontrollable sobbing, and clung to him, resting her forehead against his chest. It was a while before she could get any words out.

'Am I really that pigheaded?' she said, half laughing.

He nodded and a strange, surprised chuckle accompanied his answer. 'Yes.'

She looked up at his head again. He didn't need to say another word. In his normal, efficient way he'd found the perfect way to communicate with her. She knew exactly why he'd done what he'd done, and precisely how much he'd been willing to put on the line for her.

She couldn't let him do it. She couldn't let him drag himself down to her level.

'You can't go to the reception like that. You'll be a laughing stock. No one will remember the exhibition. All they will see—and all they will remember— is a certifiably insane pink-headed lord! You'll never live it down.'

His arms came round her to hold her tight. 'As long as you remembered how much I love you, I wouldn't care.'

She kissed him, long and slow and sweet. 'OK, OK. I think I get the point. Now can we please go back to the cottage and do something about your hair? I've got some dye in my bathroom cabinet.'

'You think we should go with matching fire-engine red?'

'Lord Radcliffe! This is no time for you to develop an inappropriate sense of humour! I meant brown. I'll even dye mine to match if that's what you want.'

He smiled at her and her heart turned to jelly. 'OK, brown it is. But you can keep yours any colour you want.'

She handed him the hat and he pulled it back over his head. 'I'm thinking that brown maybe isn't so bad anyway. After all, it *is* the colour of chocolate. Just let me sort yours out first. I don't want you to spoil everything we've worked for just so you can get my attention. You've got it. Always.'

He gave her one of those looks that travelled right through her eyes and down into his soul. 'Now, about *always*…'

He pulled a small velvet box from his trouser pocket.

'I've been wandering around the gardens, plucking up courage and trying to work out what to say. I brought this along for inspiration.'

Josie wanted to say that he didn't have to say anything but, unfortunately, she was speechless herself. He opened the box and pulled out the most beautiful opal ring. She looked at him in amazement.

'How did you know I loved opals?'

He kissed her and pulled back, still holding her stubborn little chin in his hand. 'It's full of a thousand different colours. I figured you'd never get bored with it.'

EPILOGUE

IN THE orchard, crisp snow balanced on every branch, making it look magical.

Josie sighed and leant against Will, relishing the warmth of his torso against her back. His arms circled her and, as he kissed the side of her neck, his hands stroked the mound of her stomach, so round now she could no longer do up the last two buttons on her coat. More than ever, this orchard was her favourite place in the world.

Hattie ran in and out of the trees, circling each one and leaving a trail of footprints as she skipped a pattern in the snow.

Last autumn, when she and Will had got married, they'd held the reception here. It had just been family and a few friends, nothing grand, but Will had surprised her by winding plain white fairy lights round every single branch. Even her mother had admitted it looked very pretty. And in the twilight, as they'd waltzed under the trees, it had seemed as if the branches were covered in luminous blossom.

She sighed again and covered Will's hands with her own.

. Suddenly he jumped. 'Did you feel that? He kicked!'

She smiled and nodded. 'Do you think I could miss that? While you were feeling the feet, I was much more aware of the head bouncing on my bladder. You'd better hurry up and tell me why you dragged me out here on this absolutely freezing afternoon.'

'Look!' He removed one hand from her pregnant belly and pointed to the far end of the orchard. 'I hope they survive this sudden cold snap.'

'New trees?'

Slipping out of his arms, she walked over to the row of saplings, little more than large twigs poking out of the ground. She ran her fingers over the smooth young bark of the closest one.

'Will, I know you made a New Year's resolution to try and be a bit impulsive, but why did you buy apple trees? We have a whole orchard-full already.'

'It's our gift to Elmhurst, something to mark the start of our history together here—and a reminder...' he reached forward and tucked a strand of chocolate-brown hair behind her ear '...that, even though you look a little more like the rest of us on the outside, you are still wonderfully unique on the inside.'

'A reminder? What are we going to do? Tie knots in the trunks?'

He laughed and pulled her into his arms. 'They're a special variety. A cross between Lady William and Golden Delicious.'

She gave him a look, one eyebrow raised.

Will grinned and placed the softest, sweetest kiss on the tip of her nose then whispered in her ear, 'Pink Ladies.'